Super

AARON DIETZ

Emergency Press
New York

Book design and cover by Charlie Potter
Documents H and N designed by Kristen Mullin Bakken

Cataloging-in-Publication Data
Dietz, Aaron
    Super / Aaron Dietz.
        236 p.   21 cm.
    ISBN 978-0-9753623-9-6
    1. Experimental fiction, American. 2. Heroes – Fiction.
3. Wit and humor. 4. Psychological fiction.
5. Self-realization – Fiction. 6. Social perception – Fiction.

813.0108054 –dc22

Printed in the United States of America
Published by Emergency Press
emergencypress.org

10   9   8   7   6   5   4   3   2   1

Inquire within

Application for Employment

Pike County Super Services Div.

Position Applied For:
Contract-to-Hire Superhero

Note: Applicants must be willing to work evening, night, and weekend hours.

Name:

| Last | First | Middle |

Note: Use your real name. A Superhero trainer will help you in the selection of your official Superhero name.

Address:

Street

| City | State / Province | Postal Code | Country |

Note: The Pike County Super Services Division is committed to protecting your privacy. For information about how your name, address, and other personal information are protected, refer to the Privacy Policy handout available from the Department of Superhuman Resources.

Phone Number:

| Primary | Secondary |

Education

	Name	Dates	Subject	Diploma / Degree
High School				
College				
Other				
Other				

Application Z5A

Seminars, Additional Training, and Superhero Camps

Name	Dates	Subject	Certificate

Employment History

Position: _____ Dates: _____

Company: _____ Salary: _____

Primary Duties: _____

Reason for Leaving: _____

Position: _____ Dates: _____

Company: _____ Salary: _____

Primary Duties: _____

Reason for Leaving: _____

Position: _____ Dates: _____

Company: _____ Salary: _____

Primary Duties: _____

Reason for Leaving: _____

Skills Checklist

- ☐ Word processing
- ☐ Typing:
  ____ words per minute
- ☐ Quick change:
  ____ seconds changing out of and into one outfit
- ☐ Presentation software
- ☐ Spreadsheet software
- ☐ Computer programming
- ☐ Public speaking
- ☐ Customer service
- ☐ Grant writing
- ☐ Project management
- ☐ Teaching and/or training
- ☐ Flying
- ☐ Super strength
- ☐ Other:

_____

_____

Additional Skills, Super Powers, Language Fluencies, and Other Relevant Knowledge

- ☐ _____
- ☐ _____
- ☐ _____
- ☐ _____
- ☐ _____
- ☐ _____

Submit your application, cover letter, and contact information for three references to the Department of Superhuman Resources at the Hall of Humanity.

The Hall of Humanity is an equal opportunity employer.

Pike County Super Services Division

Dear Prospective Superhero,

Congratulations! This is an official invitation for you to join the team. We believe that your skills, knowledge, and experience will enable you to make a strong contribution.

General terms of employment follow:

1. Your employment depends on passing a physical exam, to be administered within the next seven days.
2. The position you have been hired for is: Level 0 Superhero.
3. Your salary will be $_____ per hour.
4. This is a contract-to-hire position that lasts for a period of 90 days. At the end of your contract period, the Pike County Super Services Division may or may not request you to test for the position of Level I Superhero, a salaried position with full Superhero benefits.

Over →

The Super Services Division looks forward to working with you in providing Superhero services to our vast clientele.

Sincerely,

Pike County Super Services Division,
Director of Super Services

I accept the above
offer of employment: _____

Print your name: _____

Date: _____

Non-Disclosure Agreement

I agree not to disclose information relating to:

1. The secret identities, residences, and personal information of Superheroes.
2. Weaknesses of Superheroes.
3. Methods, tactics, and secret abilities used by Superheroes for the fighting of crime and saving of worlds and other environments.

I agree to take extra-reasonable precautions to protect such information.

Signature: _____

Date: _____

Orientation Checklist

Your orientation will include the location of the following:
- ☐ Break room
- ☐ Vending machines
- ☐ Coffee shop
- ☐ Cafeteria
- ☐ Locker room and assigned locker
- ☐ Computer lab
- ☐ Where to get time sheets
- ☐ Where to turn in time sheets

You will receive the following materials and handouts during your orientation:
- ☐ Superhero Handbook
- ☐ Locker Room Rules
- ☐ Computer Lab Rules
- ☐ Science Lab Rules
- ☐ Your patrol schedule
- ☐ An Explanation of Neighborhood Markings document
- ☐ A set of keys (roof access to all buildings on your patrol)

During your first day as a Superhero, you must sign up for the following information sessions:
- ☐ Super Benefits Package Discussion
- ☐ Super Retirement Planning 101
- ☐ Super Sexual Harassment and You (video session)
- ☐ Super Cultural Awareness and Sensitivity (video session)
- ☐ Planning Your Superhero Name and Costume
- ☐ Your Fans Could Get You Killed: How to Manage Your Fan Base for Maximum Exposure AND Safety!
- ☐ Your Secret Identity* and You (optional for those not intending to maintain a secret identity)

Your Superhero trainer will help you get started on:

- Creating your Superhero name.
- Planning your costume.

Keep in mind that your Superhero name and costume are subject to approval by:

- The Superhero Historian.
- A panel of Level VII or higher Superheroes.
- The Extra-Sensitivity Committee.
- The Public Relations and Marketing Department.
- The County Commissioner.

*Secret identities are mandatory for those that opt out of the Headquarters Residency package, paid for by 32% of your salary.

Explanation of Neighborhood Markings

The Pike County Super Services Division has implemented a county-wide official markings and descriptive symbols action plan. Knowing these markings and symbols will assist you during your neighborhood patrol.

Height of Building

The height of buildings indicates the vertical distance between the rooftop and ground level, marked for those with unusual leaping ability.

Distance of Leap between Buildings

The distance and angle of the jump are indicated. A negative angle indicates a jump from a taller building to a shorter building.

Stairway with Access to Roof

Use these stairways to get to the roof of buildings in your neighborhood.

Titanium-Reinforced Spring-Loaded Awning

Use these titanium-reinforced, spring-loaded awnings to break your fall when you need to transport yourself from a rooftop or other high location to ground level in a short amount of time.

Recommended Battle Zone

Whenever possible, shift the location of combat to Recommended Battle Zone areas. Recommended Battle Zone areas are areas that have a decreased likelihood of civilian casualties and a stronger chance of minimizing property damage.

Superhero Name and Costume Planning Sheet

Your Superhero trainer and the official Superhero tailor can help you plan your costume. After submitting your design, it will be considered for approval by various entities.

Any brand name endorsements or visible brand labels must be requested in a separate form (Costume Modification Form 1A23).

Proposed Superhero Name: _____

Attach three views of your Superhero costume design for approval. Specify material and color where applicable. We recommend materials that stretch.

Write a brief statement about any deliberate meaning behind the design.

_____

_____

_____

_____

☐ I certify that I have the legal right to use this design.

The Superhero Historian will check your name and costume design for any past Superhero name or costume design that is identical or too similar.

This costume has been approved by:

_____

Superhero Historian   Date

_____

Panel review representative   Date

_____

Extra-Sensitivity Committee   Date

_____

Public Relations and Marketing Department   Date

_____

County Commissioner   Date

Once your Superhero name and costume are approved, and the costume is produced and tailored, a welcome luncheon and press conference will be scheduled for you to meet the public and announce your existence as an official Superhero.

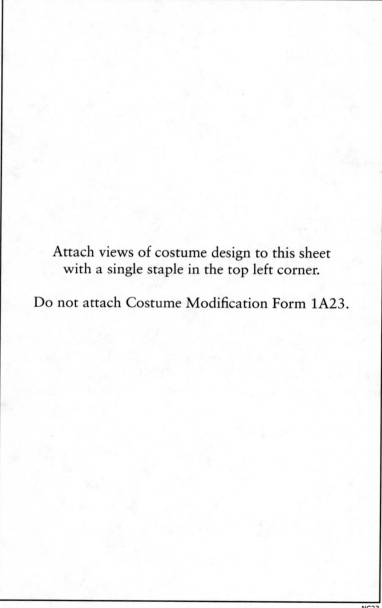

Attach views of costume design to this sheet
with a single staple in the top left corner.

Do not attach Costume Modification Form 1A23.

NC23

Level I: Might
Examination for Promotion
EXFP-LVI

PCSSJ

Pike County Super Services Div.

You are taking the Level I Examination for Promotion because the Pike County Super Services Division has determined that there is a need for a Level I Superhero. You have successfully passed the screening process, interview, and training period.

After a brief skills review, you'll need to successfully complete three live simulation test scenarios and the Level I Psychological Assessment in order to be promoted to Level I.

Skills Review
Review the skills you focused on in training before continuing.

Your Level I Superhero training focused on:

- Quiet neighborhoods during the day.
- Villain encounters of less than five minutes.
- Heights.
- Weight training.
- Punching.
- Sewing and costume repair.

Introduction to Scenarios

During your Level I training, your trainer will introduce
you to the VCR (Virtual Combat Room). It runs virtual
interactive combat scenarios, records them, and plays them
back for analysis. Though you may feel pain and experience
serious injury and/or death during VCR sessions, those
experiences will only be simulations.

You are required to pass all three VCR scenarios before
moving on to the Level I Psychological Assessment. For each
scenario, a passing grade is 70 points.

Scenario 1: The Brick Wall
Objective: Break out of the brick enclosure.

Points		
	100	Escape within 5 seconds
	90	Escape within 1:00 minute
	80	Escape within 3:00 minutes
	70	Escape within 5:00 minutes
10 bonus points awarded for avoiding personal injury		

Scenario 2: The Fall
Objective: Survive the fall off of the 30-story building.

Points		
	100	Survival, no serious injuries
	85	Survival, serious injuries but not in critical condition
	70	Survival, in critical condition, not mortally wounded
10 bonus points awarded for being in free fall within 5 seconds		
10 bonus points awarded for not touching the window sills or wall		

Scenario 3: The Mighty Villain

Objective: Render the villain unconscious. No points will be awarded if the villain is killed or mortally wounded.

	100	The villain is unconscious within 10 seconds
Points	90	The villain is unconscious within 1:00 minute
	80	The villain is unconscious within 3:00 minutes
	70	The villain is unconscious within 5:00 minutes
10 bonus points awarded for avoiding personal injury		

Introduction to the Psychological Assessment
EXFP-LVI-C

The Pike County Super Services Division recognizes the extreme duress that Superheroes at all levels are exposed to. In order to be successful at each successive level of employment, an extra-sound mind is imperative. Thus, the Pike County Super Services Division and the Pike County Super Psychology Taskforce have assembled a comprehensive psychological assessment for each level of employment.

Level I Psychological Assessment

The Level I Psychological Assessment is given on the following pages. There is no time limit for completion of this assessment, but the length of time you take will be recorded and considered along with your responses.

Directions

Read Documents A and B, and then answer the related questions. There are no right or wrong answers.

Grading

The Super Services Division will evaluate your responses with guidance from a panel of peers at Level IV or higher. A passing grade will be acknowledged with a pay increase and official promotion to Level I duties.

Record the date and time before you begin.

Year	Month	Day	Hour	Minute	AM/PM

Document A

Jake

I confess to the mannequin: "I've taken the day off to shop with Gloria."

"I told them I was sick."

"You understand, don't you?"

The mannequin understands.

"My name is Jake."

I hold out my hand, but the mannequin doesn't want to shake.

Nearby, one of the sales people puts a lot of energy into dressing a mannequin torso (headless and armless).

Gloria says,
"Small...
small...
small...
small...."

A tall man walks by wearing a long coat. Clearly he has brought a machine gun to the mall and is about to kill us all. I quickly plan out how I am going to back flip through the air to land behind the marble pillar where I can then grab the metal pole out of the clothes rack and rush the tall man with it. I'll pole vault over to him. He'll think I just flew out of the sky and I'll rap him on the head with the big metal pole. Then I'll take his gun away and he'll be unconscious and everyone will be okay. Naturally, I'll do this not because I want to be a hero but because it's my nature. It's what I do. It can't be helped. I get ready.

The tall man leaves the store.

Gloria says, "Ooh! Large!"

She takes her things to the fitting room and I wait.

Document B

Irma

"Hold still, Paper. I'm almost done."

Irma held the sheet of paper down.

As she added an orange streak to the sky, a purple crayon jumped out of the box and covered the picture with swirling lines.

"Stop it, Purple! You're ruining my drawing!"

She grabbed the crayon and stuffed it back in the box.

"Now, don't let anything out unless I tell you to," she told the box. She looked at the picture and sighed.

"Oh well. I can make another one tomorrow," she said. "You can go now, Paper."

The sheet of paper scrambled off the desk, out of the room, and down the hall.

"Okay, Radio. That's enough music."

A button marked play popped up.

"Come on, Watch. Let's go."

A watch crawled across the desk and wrapped itself around her wrist. Irma looked out the window at the courtyard below.

"Purple Crayon is going crazy," she said, stroking the watch, "and Tire's been playing rough again."

Irma left the room and started down one of the many flights of stairs in the abandoned building.

"Things just go crazy sometimes. That's why all the people left. All they had to do was scold things once in a while, but they were too afraid." She sighed.

The watch gently squeezed her wrist as she headed down a hallway.

When she reached a swinging door, she pounded on it. It didn't move.

"Come on. Open up!"

Pushing up on her toes, she stretched to see through the circular window.

"Let me in!"

She hit the door again.

"Soon I'll be big enough to see in the window, and then I'll find out what's going on in there!"

She slumped to the floor.

"Come on, Door. Please?"

The door didn't move.

She stood and kicked it hard.

Plodding down the last of the stairs, Irma looked at the watch. Its hands moved erratically, randomly changing direction.

Irma stepped out of the building. She spotted the tire leaning against the jungle gym at the far side of the courtyard.

"Tire! I need to talk to you."

The tire rose and rolled slowly over to Irma.

"I'm sorry for scolding you yesterday."

The tire came closer so she could pet it.

"I know you didn't mean to hurt me, and I shouldn't have been so angry with you."

The tire bounced a little under her tiny, soft hand. Across the courtyard, a door opened. A cart rolled out, carrying a tray.

"Yum, chicken!" Irma exclaimed. "Thank you, Cart. Jungle Jim! I need a place to sit."

The jungle gym maneuvered its numerous, skeleton-like legs of pipe across the courtyard. After planting itself in the ground near Irma, its long, steel arms formed a seat of bars.

"Thank you," she said. As she sat, a warm rubbery surface nudged her leg.

"Not now, Tire. We'll play later."

She grabbed a chicken leg and bit into it. She drew a massive chunk of meat and skin into her mouth and chewed slowly. She frowned, and then quickly plucked the mangled piece of leg from her mouth with her finger.

"Yuck! The chicken tastes funny again."

She set the fleshy bone down on the plate. She finished a side of cooked vegetables and ate the chocolate pudding.

"Thank you. The chicken tasted bad again, but everything else was okay."

The cart took the remains of the meal away.

"Thanks for the seat, Jungle Jim."

She got up and patted its cold, hard surface.

"Want to play tag with me and Tire?"

The jungle gym shuddered.

"I know, I know. You're too slow. That's okay. I'll play with you later."

To the tire, she shouted, "You're it!" She slapped it and sprinted across the grass. The tire sprung after her, but she made it to the building and shut the door.

"Don't let Tire in until you count to twenty," she ordered.

The door remained closed as the tire bounced into it, slamming against its hollow steel. A metallic ring echoed through the halls of the building.

Irma ran up several flights of stairs and into a hallway. She crawled under a desk at the far end of a room.

Minutes later she heard the tire rolling down the hall, checking each room. Finally, it entered and moved past several rows of desks. When she heard it fall on its side to check for her feet, she knew she was discovered.

She leaped out of her hiding spot in a blind run. The tire bounded after her, jumping over desks in its way. A final jump struck her, sending her flying head first into the wall.

Irma woke up with a strong headache and a skinned knee. She could hear the tire careening down the stairs as she stumbled to the first aid room.

There, the box of bandages wouldn't open.

"Open, Box!" she shouted. "I say open!"

Crying, she slammed it repeatedly on the counter until it spit out two bandages. She stuck them on her knee.

Since she didn't trust the elevator to take her to the correct floor anymore, she limped down the stairs.

The tire stood in the far corner of the courtyard. When it saw Irma, it approached her, rolling across the brown, dying grass.

"You get away from me, Tire! I don't want to play with you anymore."

The tire continued rolling.

She turned and walked around the building quickly. The tire followed.

Out in front of the building, desolate structures of concrete and steel surrounded her.

She reached a sidewalk and spun to face the tire, unaware of the dark blood trickling down the side of her head.

"I told you to leave me alone! Get away!" she cried. She turned and walked faster. But the tire sped up and was closer when she turned around again.

"No!" she shrieked. "Get away from me!"

She ran, but the tire kept up by bouncing. As Irma looked over her shoulder at the black circle of rubber flying through the air, she let out a scream.

Level I

Psychological Assessment Questions

Form **2410-138**
RC3-990178

Name:	ID:
County: **Pike County**	Date:

How to fill out this form:
- For multiple choice questions, completely fill the box to the left of your choice.
- For write-in answers, please print legibly in the space provided.

In Document A, what size is Gloria looking for?
- ☐ Small.
- ☐ Medium.
- ☐ Large.
- ☐ Extra Large.
- ☐ She doesn't know what size she's looking for.
- ☐ She's not looking for a size.

In Document A, is the tall man in a long coat a villain?
- ☐ Yes.
- ☐ No.
- ☐ There is not enough information to figure it out.

In Document B, where are all the other people?
- ☐ They have been killed by a villain.
- ☐ The tire killed them accidentally.
- ☐ Irma killed them.
- ☐ They are retired.
- ☐ They were destroyed by science.
- ☐ Other:

_____

_____

In Document B, what do you think is going on behind the swinging door?

_____

_____

List three things that Irma, from Document B, is unaware of.

_____

_____

_____

Of the characters from Documents A and B, which of them is the most mighty?
- ☐ Gloria.
- ☐ Irma.
- ☐ Jake.
- ☐ The tall man in a long coat.
- ☐ The tire.

Explain your answer to the previous question.

_____

_____

_____

_____

Form 2410-138

Continued on other side

Please do not write in this space.

Form 2410-138

Level II: Beauty
Examination for Promotion
EXFP-LVII

Pike County Super Services Div.

You are taking the Level II Examination for Promotion because the Pike County Super Services Division has determined that there is a need for a Level II Superhero. You have successfully passed the interview and you are still a potential candidate for the position.

After a brief skills review, you'll need to successfully complete three live simulation test scenarios and the Level II Psychological Assessment in order to be promoted to Level II.

Skills Review
Review the skills you focused on in training before continuing.

Your Level II Superhero training focused on:

- Quiet neighborhoods during the night.
- Staying awake for long periods of time.
- Stretches and conditioning.
- Kicking.
- Public speaking and the two minute speech.

Scenarios

You are required to pass all three VCR (Virtual Combat Room) scenarios before moving on to the Level II Psychological Assessment. For each scenario, a passing grade is 70 points.

Scenario 4: The Press Conference
Objective: Avoid or redirect questions from members of the press successfully.

Points		
	100	Zero questions answered, zero speech disfluencies
	90	Less than 10% of the questions answered, fewer than 40 speech disfluencies
	80	Less than 20% of the questions answered, fewer than 80 speech disfluencies
	70	Less than 30% of the questions answered, fewer than 120 speech disfluencies
5 bonus points awarded for each request for a date		
20 bonus points awarded for each marriage proposal		

Scenario 5: The Clerk
Objective: Convince the bank teller to give you the full transaction history for account number 15746491.

Points		
	100	Transaction history acquired within 5:00 minutes
	90	Transaction history acquired within 10:00 minutes
	80	Transaction history acquired within 20:00 minutes
	70	Transaction history acquired within 30:00 minutes
10 bonus points awarded for not telling the clerk you are a Superhero		
-50 points for using violence		

Scenario 6: The Indifferent Villain

Objective: Use inner or outer beauty to convince the villain to defuse the bomb before it explodes.

Points	100	Bomb defused within 30 seconds
	90	Bomb defused within 1:00 minute
	80	Bomb defused within 2:00 minutes
	70	Bomb defused within 3:00 minutes
-50 points for using violence		
-50 points for defusing the bomb yourself		

Level II Psychological Assessment

EXFP-LVII-C

The Level II Psychological Assessment is given on the following pages. There is no time limit for completion of this assessment, but the length of time you take will be recorded and considered along with your responses.

Directions

Read Documents C and D, and then answer the related questions. There are no right or wrong answers. A Reference Sheet has been included as an optional aid. Researching related people and events in the Hall of Humanity's archives is not allowed.

Grading

The Super Services Division will evaluate your responses with guidance from a panel of peers at Level V or higher. A passing grade will be acknowledged with a pay increase and official promotion to Level II duties.

Record the date and time before you begin.

Year	Month	Day	Hour	Minute	AM/PM

Reference Sheet

Real Name	Position
Irma	Civilian, known unregistered super-powered entity
Tamara	Civilian, masseuse
Dr. Ilona	Civilian*, doctor
Pulmo	Unregistered extraterrestrial, known unregistered super-powered entity
Nelson	Civilian**, philanthropist
Reuben	Civilian, licensed Superhero agent
Sera	Level V Superhero

*In Document D, Dr. Ilona is a Level VI Physician.
**In Document D, Nelson is a Level II Superhero.

Document C

The Shot

By Irma

I woke up. The alarms were going off again.

Tamara was staring out the window.

"I have a new power," I said.

"How do you always know?" she asked.

"I just know."

I got out of bed. I grabbed a clay mug off the dresser and dumped some earrings out of it.

"Think anyone will miss this?" I asked.

Tamara looked and shrugged.

I thought of the power of fire and the mug melted in my hand.

Tamara was still standing by the window.

"Maybe it's not a drill," I said.

It took a second for her to speak.

"Yeah," she said. "It's not a drill this time."

"How do you do it?" I asked.

"What?"

"You're always cool."

Tamara shrugged.

"Your jacket," I said, holding it up.

She smiled. "I won't need it today. What's your new super power?"

"I can melt things, but I can't do it from a distance. I have to touch them."

Tamara nodded.

"Is there a fight coming?" I asked.

"I don't know yet."

Doctor Ilona looked up as we walked by. She was locking her office, purse hanging from her shoulder.

"Pulmo said they were going to the roof," she told us. She dropped her keys.

"Thanks," Tamara said.

We went up several flights of stairs and out onto the roof. The air smelled like gas. Pulmo and Nelson were on the far side. We walked toward them, passing the swimming pool and the tennis court.

Pulmo looked at us and held a finger to his mouth. "Shh."

He pointed to the edge of the roof, and then he and Nelson got on their knees and crawled over. Their heads peeked over the waist-high stone wall.

I moved closer to look. The building was surrounded by tanks and jeeps and a thick barricade of people in uniform holding black weapons. Dr. Ilona was being escorted to a limousine just outside the ring of vehicles and soldiers.

Tamara looked at me and shook her head once, from left to right. I shut my eyes and tried to stop hyperventilating. My body wouldn't listen to me. We'd been outnumbered before, but never like this.

I opened my eyes and looked at Tamara again. She was calm. My breathing slowed.

Then a blast of air flew by and Tamara fell back. Nelson jerked me down, his shoulder knocking the wind out of me when we landed.

I turned my head and saw Pulmo holding his cape against Tamara's shoulder. The cape was turning dark red.

Nelson got off me and whispered to Tamara, "Are you okay?"

She didn't answer, but she seemed alert. I wanted to say, "She can't hear you," but I couldn't breathe.

Tamara looked at me. My head hurt and there was a loud rushing sound in my ears drowning out my thoughts.

Gradually, the noise faded and I could hear my heart pumping blood to my head. Air flowed into my lungs. I heard Nelson ask Tamara again, "Are you okay?" Then he said it again and I realized he was shouting. He had been all along.

I sat up. The sound of my pulse got louder and louder and soon Nelson looked up. He heard it, too.

"Choppers," he said. He was right. I wasn't hearing my pulse. It was the sound of helicopters.

Suddenly I felt fine.

I grabbed Tamara's ankles. Pulmo grabbed her shoulders and we picked her up together. Nelson jogged ahead, looking out for the helicopters.

"Four members of this super-powered team and not one of us can levitate stuff," Pulmo said.

"Hey, you're the alien," Nelson said. "Shouldn't you have a levitation device or something?"

"I'll have to work on that."

We carried Tamara across the tennis court and past the swimming pool. A tennis ball floated in the water.

I moved my hand along the doorframe, fusing the door to the wall.

"There. It will take them a while to get in," I said.

Nelson grabbed his communicator off his utility belt.

"What are you doing?" Pulmo asked.

"I'm calling Reuben," Nelson said. "Hopefully he can stop them from killing us."

Pulmo looked at me, and then said, "Nelson, it's not right to have to ask permission to use our powers."

"Of course it's not right, but you're either dead or an officially recognized Superhero. And I'm making the choice for you. Reuben might be a sleazy Superhero agent, but he's our only hope of getting out of this alive."

"You'll be enlisted, too," Pulmo said. "They'll get all of us."

"I actually prefer that over dying at the hands of a scary team of professionals trained in taking down illegal Superheroes. You're all so damned loyal to each other you're going to get each other killed."

"Pulmo," I said, "I wouldn't be alive right now if it weren't for your help. I'll do whatever you want."

"It wouldn't change the core of what we do," Pulmo said. "We can't help people if we're dead."

"Right. I understand."

I sat on the carpet, next to Tamara. She was unconscious, but breathing strong. I checked the bandage on her shoulder.

Nelson said, "If I live through this, I'm becoming a film producer."

"A waste of your powers," Pulmo said.

The communicator beeped. "Nelson," a voice said.

"Reuben," Nelson answered. "We need some help and we need it fast."

I looked at Tamara.

"If I live through this," I said, "I'm going to keep doing the same thing we're doing."

Document D

A Hastily Written Film Synopsis Proposal Thing

By Nelson

The quick pitch, in case I run out of time:

1. The doctor gives me six months to live.
2. I fall in love with Sera.
3. I shrink.

If this were a movie, I'd want it to feel like measuring the coastline of an island. When you look at the coast from a distance, it appears to have a certain measurement, a certain distance around. But as you get closer, you realize that each section that appeared reasonably straight from a distance is made up of tinier and tinier inlets and curves and distractions. Your theoretical measurement of the coastline gets larger and larger the closer you get to the water. And so on, for eternity.

I'm delaying the inevitable, which isn't like me. I asked the doctor to tell it to me straight and she did. I took it pretty well. I got out of my Level II Superhero position before my shoes were back on. Since I had nothing to lose anymore, I went straight to a bombed out building in the middle of downtown, where Sera was distributing blankets, and I asked her out.

Soon after, she found out that I was dying. Since we were on short time, we spent every possible moment together. She took a leave from work. I quit everything. We even avoided being in separate rooms. Sometimes at night I'd get up for a glass of water, but I'd come back to drink it next to her.

We had a semi-normal relationship for the first two months. Then, Sera started to have to do things for me. Simple stuff at first, like getting stuff from the tall cupboards, or lifting the heavy grocery bags. Eventually, she did everything, from cooking to turning on the TV.

Sera didn't complain when I wasn't able to put my arm around her at night. Instead, she'd pull me into her arms and hold me as if I were a child.

For a while, we hoped Doc Ilona could keep the disease from getting too debilitating. But after baffling Ilona and several other specialists, we didn't waste any more time on doctors. With three months to go before I was gone, I decided to spend the time entirely on Sera.

When it became too dangerous for Sera to touch me, we had to be satisfied with staring at each other. She'd say the most loving things to me, but by that time my voice was too quiet for her to hear.

When it was close to the end, we
came up with a plan. In order
for me to keep getting food and
water, we built a small shelter
about a centimeter high that
served as my home. Whenever it
got dark, I went under the shelter
so Sera could change my food and
water without drowning me or
crushing me with a breadcrumb.
Sometimes the water was salty.

Eventually, the smooth surface
of the table grew into mountains
and valleys. I quit going back to
the shelter and slept nearer to
the food, since each day it was
a longer hike between the two
points. I didn't have to worry
about getting crushed anymore
because now there were great
valleys with caves to hide in.

Finally, I became so
light that the wind
picked me up. I flew
out the window trying
hard not to look at the
sun, the only object
that didn't seem any
larger to me.

I continued shrinking,
discovering new worlds
regularly, but they
were fleeting and often
forgotten as soon as I
shrank out of them.

Level II

Name:	ID:
County: **Pike County**	Date:

How to fill out this form:
- For multiple choice questions, completely fill the box to the left of your choice.
- For write-in answers, please print legibly in the space provided.
- For matching questions, draw a line from an item on the left to an item on the right.

Use the information in Document C to match each person with their super power.

Irma   Ability to tell when someone is lying
Tamara   Ability to see the future
Pulmo   Ability to melt matter
Nelson   Resistance to all earthborn disease

Explain your choices for the super powers of Tamara, Pulmo, and Nelson.

_____

_____

_____

In Document C, why does Irma appreciate Tamara's calm demeanor? Check all that apply.
- ☐ Irma craves stability in her life.
- ☐ Irma is romantically interested in Tamara.
- ☐ Irma is scared.
- ☐ Irma has no other female role models.
- ☐ Other:

_____

_____

_____

Name the medical condition that affects the narrator of Document D.
- ☐ Dementia.
- ☐ Exaggerated bone loss.
- ☐ Low self esteem.
- ☐ Love.
- ☐ An unnamed shrinking disease.
- ☐ There is not enough information to figure it out.

In Document D, why was Sera willing to care for the narrator, Nelson?
- ☐ She enjoyed his appreciation of her beauty.
- ☐ She cares for everyone.
- ☐ Nelson was beautiful.
- ☐ Nelson was rich.
- ☐ Nelson had a sense of humor.
- ☐ Other:

Continued on other side

Of the characters from Documents C and D, which of them is the most beautiful?
- ☐ Dr. Ilona
- ☐ Irma
- ☐ Nelson
- ☐ Pulmo
- ☐ Reuben
- ☐ Sera
- ☐ Tamara

Explain your answer to the previous question.

_____
_____
_____
_____
_____
_____

Please do not write in this space.

Level III: Athleticism
Examination for Promotion
EXFP-LVIII

Pike County Super Services Div.

You are taking the Level III Examination for Promotion because the Pike County Super Services Division has determined that there is a need for a Level III Superhero. You have successfully passed the interview and you are still a potential candidate for the position.

After a brief skills review, you'll need to successfully complete three live simulation test scenarios and the Level III Psychological Assessment in order to be promoted to Level III.

Skills Review
Review the skills you focused on in training before continuing.

Your Level III Superhero training focused on:

- Active neighborhoods during the day.
- Villain encounters of less than ten minutes.
- Gymnastics.
- Creative fighting.

Scenarios
EXFP-LVIII-B

You are required to pass all three VCR (Virtual Combat Room) scenarios before moving on to the Level III Psychological Assessment. For each scenario, a passing grade is 70 points.

Scenario 7: The Pickup Game
Objective: Win the basketball game by at least 2 points.

Points	100	Hold the opponents to 0 points
	90	Win by 8 points or more
	80	Win by 4 points or more
	70	Win by 2 points or more
20 bonus points awarded for not using any super powers		
5 bonus points awarded for each dunk		
1 bonus point awarded for each rebound, block, steal, or assist		
-10 points for each player injured		
-20 points for each player put in critical condition		
-50 points for using ability-enhancing drugs		

Scenario 8: The Delivery

Objective: Deliver the groceries to apartment number 1910, on the nineteenth floor of 24 West 71st Ave.

Points	100	Deliver 100% of the items within 1:00 minute
	90	Deliver 100% of the items within 4:00 minutes
	80	Deliver 90% of the items within 6:00 minutes
	70	Deliver 80% of the items within 8:00 minutes
20 bonus points awarded for not using any super powers		
-5 points for each broken egg		
-5 points for each spilled container of liquid		
-5 points for not keeping the cold items together in the bag		

Scenario 9: The Athletic Villain

Objective: Chase and apprehend the villain through the crowded street. No points will be awarded if the villain is killed or mortally wounded.

Points	100	Caught within 30 seconds
	90	Caught within 2:00 minutes
	80	Caught within 4:00 minutes
	70	Caught within 6:00 minutes
-5 points for tripping over an obstacle		
-5 points for each civilian who is hurt		
-50 points for each civilian who is killed or mortally wounded		

Level III Psychological Assessment
EXFP-LVIII-C

The Level III Psychological Assessment is given on the following pages. There is no time limit for completion of this assessment, but the length of time you take will be recorded and considered along with your responses.

Directions

Read Documents E and F, and then answer the related questions. There are no right or wrong answers. A Reference Sheet has been included as an optional aid. Researching related people and events in the Hall of Humanity's archives is allowed with written permission from a Level VIII or higher Superhero, but the information will not help you.

Grading

The Super Services Division will evaluate your responses with guidance from a panel of peers at Level VI or higher. A passing grade will be acknowledged with a pay increase and official promotion to Level III duties.

Record the date and time before you begin.

Year	Month	Day	Hour	Minute	AM/PM

Reference Sheet

EXFP-LVIII-D

Real Name	Superhero Name	Position
Irma	Protea	Level III Superhero*
Robert	Alabaster Wight**	Civilian***, shelver
Tamara	Tamara	Level IV Superhero
Jake	N/A	Civilian, nature guide
Auslander	Auslander	Level VII Superhero
Vergiften	N/A	Class C villain
Maya	N/A	Level II Administrative Assistant
Praxis	Praxis	Level X Superhero
Carver	Moonclaw	Level 0 Contract Superhero

*In Document F, Irma is a Level V Superhero.
**In Document E, Robert has no Superhero name.
***In Document F, Robert is a Level II Superhero.

Document E

Altitude

There was a stranger below.

Irma watched him set his pack down, crouch next to the tape player, then reach out and tilt it back a little.

He let it continue playing.

He looked around, then up into the trees, but he didn't spot her.

She watched him lean back on the grass and close his eyes.

After she heard him snoring, she moved.

Irma stepped off the tree branch and let herself fall. She grabbed a branch ten feet off the ground and swung under and up, letting go when her inertia was ready to carry her back up into the sky.

She pivoted in the air, and then came to rest on top of a branch right above the stranger.

She hopped to the ground.

Robert woke up under her shadow.

"Can I have my tape player?" she asked.

He looked around.

"Sorry," he said. "I saw it there and decided to listen. I must have dozed off."

The tape player was playing the song that had been in his dream.

"Thanks for not running off with it," she said. "I was climbing a tree."

"Pretty odd, having a tape player in the middle of the forest."

She blinked.

"Or at all, really," he said.

"How far are you going?" she asked.

"Down to Gisborne."

"How far is that?"

"About six kilometers."

He smiled. "I'm Robert," he said.

"Irma."

She sat and watched him pull a map out of his pack.

"You carried a tape player all the way out here?" he asked.

She shook her head, and then pointed at his map. "My friend and I work here sometimes. It's not far."

"That's government land. What do you do?"

"There's...sort of a lab there. The government lets us use it."

"What kind of lab?"

She shrugged. "It's really my friend's specialty. I'm mostly just hanging out."

He folded up the map. "You got dragged out here while your friend works?"

"I wanted to get away for a while."

"Understandable."

She looked at her watch. "Look, I better go. I'm supposed to meet her soon."

He stood as she picked up the tape player.

"You want to come with?" she asked.

Robert and Irma sat on the hood of a car. The smooth, silver government building obscured the sun, and the same tape of music was repeating itself for the third time.

"I should get going I guess," Robert said.

"I'm sorry. She thought she'd be done by seven."

"That's okay. I just need to find a good flat spot to sleep for the night."

"What time do you have to be in Gisborne?"

"Tomorrow afternoon. It won't be hard."

"Listen, you could stay in Macedon tonight and we could drive you up tomorrow. You could probably get a spot in the same hostel as us."

He thought for a moment. "Are you sure your friend won't mind driving me?"

"Absolutely."

"And we can hang out, then, tonight?"

"Of course."

"All right then."

Soon, a woman came out of the building fidgeting with sunglasses. As she flipped her hair back to put the glasses on, she spotted Robert on the hood of her car.

"Picked up a stray?" she asked.

She introduced herself while driving.

"Tamara," she said.

"Robert," he said. He shook Tamara's hand from the back seat.

Tamara frowned at him in the rearview mirror. "That's funny. You actually look like a Robert."

"Good. Now I know what Roberts look like," he said.

"What is it that you do, Robert?"

"What does it look like I do?"

"It looks like you spend your time hitching rides from the friends of overly-generous women."

"That's right," Robert said, emphasizing his speech with a pointed finger. "That's exactly right."

"Robert," Tamara said, "I can tell you are trouble."

"He wasn't trouble when I found him," Irma said. "Of course, he was sleeping at the time."

In Macedon, Robert stashed his pack at the hostel and then insisted on buying a bottle of wine to go with dinner.

Tamara said, "Make it a good bottle of wine then."

"Anything is fine with me," Irma said. "He can buy the food, too."

They laughed.

Tamara and Irma hooked arms. Robert followed them up the street to the local grill. Outside the door, they could smell spices cooked in flame.

Robert's next flash of coherent thought came while he was throwing up.

"I didn't have to buy so much wine."

"Yes, well, you're a regular nuisance," Tamara said.

"It was very nice of you to get that third bottle," Irma said. She used a tissue to dab at some saliva dripping from Robert's chin.

"The fourth was a bit desperate," Tamara said.

He stood up and they walked him out of the restroom.

"Was the food any good?" he asked. Then he hit the floor.

Robert was still in his cot. He could hear Tamara and Irma's laughter approaching from down the street. A screen door slammed, and soon they were holding food in front of him.

"We got you breakfast," Irma said. "It's still warm."

He took bread from her hand and bit into it.

"More like a late lunch," said Tamara, holding up a block of cheese.

He bit off a piece.

"Are you feeling okay?" Irma asked.

He thought for a moment. "Yeah."

"No pounding in the head?" Tamara asked. She knocked her palm against his head several times.

"No," he said with his mouth full. "I feel pretty good, really."

"You must have puked it all out last night," Irma said. She put her hand on his forehead.

"Hungry," he said. He bit off more bread and a little cheese. "I definitely killed some brain cells last night, because I don't remember either of your names."

Tamara punched his shoulder.

"I'm kidding," he said. "Anyway, sorry about last night. I blame the altitude."

"It's all right," Irma said. "It's already three o'clock. Do you need us to take you to Gisborne?"

"I'd appreciate it," he said. "I'm meeting a friend there. You could join us for dinner if you want. I'll even buy the wine again."

"Sounds like another bad idea," Tamara said.

"Then it's settled."

Jake stood at the bar talking to a man in a long coat.

"Jake," Robert said.

Jake turned away from his conversation.

"I was wondering when you'd get here," he said. "How was your hike?"

"Fabulous," Robert said. "On the way back, I met these two."

"Tamara," Tamara said, shaking Jake's hand. "This is Irma."

They shook.

"I'm Jake," he said.

"Robert," said Robert, offering his hand to Jake.

"Jerk," Jake said. He shoved Robert a little.

"How was the Divide?" Robert asked.

"Beautiful," Jake said. "I have photos. I'll send you some."

"Was there room in the hostel?"

"Sure, it's still the off season."

"We may not stay," Tamara said.

"Then we'll simply cancel your reservations in a few hours," Jake said.

"We have reservations?" Irma asked.

"I know I do," Tamara said.

"I called while you were getting gas," Robert explained.

Jake led everyone out the back onto a deck overlooking a lush ravine. They found a table and filled their stomachs while a breeze brought fresh air from the surrounding mountains.

The plates had been cleared away hours ago, but wine bottles continued to multiply.

Irma stood up and walked over to the railing. Robert joined her.

"So, what is it that you do?" he said.

"I'm an accountant," she said. "A boring accountant. You?"

"I'm an importer / exporter."

"Really?"

"No."

She laughed. "I'm not really an accountant."

Irma looked over the railing into the dark.

Robert moved to kiss her but she put her hand up.

Jake and Tamara joined them at the railing, kissing sloppily.

"I say, I'm a little tight," Jake said, imitating a British character from a Hemingway novel. He nipped at Tamara's neck.

Irma didn't pay any attention.

"I say," Jake said again, "I'm a little tight."

He tipped his glass back and frowned.

"It's empty," Tamara said.

"Easily remedied," Jake said. He spun her back to the table to pour.

Robert swallowed the rest of his wine. He turned toward the bar, but Irma grabbed his arm.

"Hey," she said. "Where are you going?"

He frowned and nodded toward Jake and Tamara.

He filled his glass at the table, then walked inside and sat at the bar. The bottles lining the wall shimmered.

Irma sat next to him.

She grabbed a peanut and flicked it against the wall behind the bar. It bounced off the shelf, rolled in and out of a bowl, then landed in the trash.

"You know," Robert said, "I'm pretty sure I've never met an Irma before."

"We're not all that common."

"But you do seem familiar."

She pushed the dish of nuts away.

Robert said, "I liked the music on that tape, by the way."

"It's my own mix."

"It's a good mix."

"Thanks."

"Can I tell you a secret?" Irma asked.

"Sure."

She leaned over to whisper in his ear: "Sometimes I have powers that make me dangerous to everyone around me."

Robert looked at her face.

"But only sometimes," she said.

He nodded. "So, how often do you have these powers?"

"Well, I always have powers. Sometimes they're a little easier to control."

"What, like, you have a new power every day?"

"Usually for longer than that, but yeah, pretty much." He nodded.

"I had a weird childhood," she said.

"I bet."

He handed her a cashew.

She took it, and then flicked it at the ceiling fan. It shot out of the fan, bounced off of a man's head, and then landed in another man's beer glass. No one noticed.

"I've got a secret, too," Robert said.

"Okay."

He looked around the bar. The bartender was at the other end settling a tab.

"You have to hold my hand," he said.

He held out his hand.

She took it.

Irma watched his hand change color until it was a smooth alabaster. Then it turned back to his ordinary skin tone.

"It's cold," she said.

"Stone," Robert said.

"I think I can help you."

Then Tamara interrupted them. "Is she telling people about her powers again?"

Jake bumped against Robert and said, "I say, I'm a little tight."

Jake had to lean on him to stand, so they called it a night.

Robert woke up with Irma standing over him.

She pushed his hair behind his ear.

She whispered, "When I was young, I had an accident. With my powers."

He didn't say anything.

"I wouldn't be here without Pulmo, and the others have helped me, too. You'll like it. We'll talk about it tomorrow," she said.

He nodded.

Then she was gone.

Robert and Jake waved from the window as the train pulled away.

"Let me know," Irma called after him.

Robert nodded and waved.

"What was all that about?" Jake said.

Robert explained for the next 30 kilometers.

"Sounds like it's too good to be true," Jake said. "But then, you're gifted and all."

"You're pretty gifted yourself," Robert said. "I already asked about you. Irma said they'd be willing to send you to a tryout."

"Oh, come on. I don't have any super powers."

"But you've got super instincts. I've seen the way your eyes watch for every possible thing that could go wrong. The only time you're able to stop is when you're drunk."

"But I drink all the time."

"Come on, Jake. Just think about it."

"Nah. Besides, I'm thinking about going back to school."

"What for?"

"I don't think it matters. Perhaps I'll write a dissertation on tedium."

Document F

Subject: Notes from Debriefing: Auslander andAlabaster Wight vs.
        Vergiften
Attachment: AusAlaVsVe███████4.rtf
Date: March 2, ██████
Message:

Hi everyone,

Please find the notes from the last debriefing attached. For your
convenience, they're also copied and pasted below.

Looks like all of you have accepted the follow-up meeting request
scheduled for August 12██████ 3:40pm to 3:50pm.

Thanks,

Maya

Notes from the debriefing on Auslander and Alabaster Wight vs. Vergiften

Meeting Duration: 10 minutes

Personnel Present:
> Praxis (Level X Superhero)
> Auslander (Level VII Superhero) with trainee Alabaster Wight
> (Level II Superhero)
> Protea (Level V Superhero) with trainee Moonclaw (Level I
> Superhero)
> Maya (Level II Administrative Assistant)

Praxis reviews encounter.
Listed as a Grade A success because:
- Less than $400 damage to surroundings in apprehension of a
  Class C villain.
- No injuries to civilians.
- All injuries to Superhero personnel neutralized within 1 hour.

Praxis calls up security camera footage for second-by-second analysis
focused on what could be done better next time. Transcript:
Frame 1:32:04
Praxis: Is that Vergiften?

Auslander: Yeah. In this frame, he's trying to break into that building, and I'm falling from the roof next door, about to apprehend him. But, as you'll see in the next frame, he hears me falling in time to attack me.

Protea: How did he hear?

Auslander: My keys shifted and he heard them jingle a little.

Praxis: That's odd. They were rubber-banded?

Auslander: They had been, but in a previous encounter from that evening, the rubber band broke, so they were loose at this moment.

Moonclaw: You carry your keys?

Protea: He's talking about standard issue keys. We all carry them. You'll get yours. We're just short right now.

Moonclaw: No, but I mean, what are they for?

Protea: Everyone is issued a set of keys that gives them roof access to the buildings in their patrol area. Page 189 of the manual.

Moonclaw: Sorry. Should I have known that?

Protea: It's okay. It's only your second day.

Alabaster Wight: But if it had been your third day, watch out.

Moonclaw: I'm on page 158. I thought that was on pace.

Protea: Seriously, it's okay.

Praxis: Let's advance the video, please.

Frame 1:32:05

Praxis: Dear me. How did your head twist back that far?

Auslander: I'm wondering that, too. So, obviously, he heard me falling, and he had the reflexes to get his arm up there like that. I thought he might have crushed some bones at first, but after a few minutes I could breathe again.

Praxis: And where is Alabaster Wight?

Alabaster Wight: I'm right there, just off frame. We timed things pretty well, considering. I circled around so I could come up from behind him just as Auslander approached from above. And actually, I didn't notice this before, but his left hand is already going for his poison darts.

Praxis: Right you are, Alabaster Wight. And you're probably about two frames away from catching one in the throat if I remember correctly.

Alabaster Wight: That's right. I didn't expect him to have upgraded his darts so they'd be able to penetrate my skin. This was only two weeks after we first ran into him.

Praxis: I want to come back to that, but for now, let's focus on the keys, since that's how he heard you coming. It seems the broken rubber band caused the problem with the approach. Any ideas how we could do better next time?

Auslander: I've been saying we should switch to key cards for years.

Protea: We priced that and it was pretty prohibitive. We'd have to convert nearly all of the buildings in our patrolled neighborhoods. It's just way too expensive.

Auslander: Well I don't see what else there is to do.

Praxis: Alabaster Wight?

Alabaster Wight: We need keys that are quiet. We can't go sneaking around if we have metal keys on us all the time.

Praxis: That's it? No other ideas?

Protea: We could change certain key neighborhoods, pardon the pun, over to the key card system, and convert others as we appropriate funds.

Praxis: I remember the bottom line on that key card memo, and I don't think it'll ever fly, not even in smaller increments. However, I've got a cheaper solution to suggest. We've all got room in our utility belts for extra rubber bands, right?

Auslander: Um. Sure?

Protea: Sounds fine, Praxis.

Alabaster Wight: Sure, yeah.

Praxis: Problem solved.

Moonclaw: I've got a question.

Praxis: Yes?

Moonclaw: Well, Alabaster Wight almost died, am I right?

Praxis: Yes.

Alabaster Wight: That's right. But I didn't.

Moonclaw: But we've got a Level X Superhero on staff.

Praxis: That's true.

Auslander: I'm not following you.

Moonclaw: Why wasn't the Level X Superhero—

Praxis: Me, you mean.

Moonclaw: Yeah, you. Why weren't you called in? You're invulnerable, right? You could have taken care of the problem without anyone even getting hurt.

Praxis: The encounter was a Grade A success. Clearly, we didn't need a Level X Superhero on the scene.

Moonclaw: But Alabaster Wight almost died.

Praxis: He didn't die. And they were only facing a Class C villain. It would be technically impossible for me to be physically present for every Class C villain encounter. I'm the only Level X Superhero in Pike County.

Protea: Moonclaw, I know it seems weird, but we face Class C villains all the time. We almost die on a regular basis. The Level X Superheroes are busy with their own patrols, but they're also generally reserved for situations that clearly warrant a response much stronger than the ordinary.

Praxis: Good then. Well, I'm sorry to cut short this discussion, but our time's up and I want to say a few things before we go. We managed to get through two seconds of footage, and identified three areas for improvement. Auslander and Alabaster Wight, you two could be a split second better synchronized in your offensive. For that, you could review a few scenarios in the VCR and get it perfect for next time. The second area of improvement is for you, Alabaster Wight. You've got to assume your enemies are smarter than you think. And lastly, we'll all start carrying extra rubber bands.

Praxis adjourns meeting on schedule, requests follow-up meeting to continue analysis.

Action Items:
- Maya will schedule VCR session time for Auslander and Alabaster Wight.
- Maya will issue another 6th priority 10 minute meeting request to continue analysis.
- Maya will update standard issue utility belt to include five extra rubber bands.

Level III

Psychological Assessment Questions

Form **2410-140**
RC3-990182

Name:	ID:
County: **Pike County**	Date:

How to fill out this form:
- For multiple choice questions, completely fill the box to the left of your choice.
- For write-in answers, please print legibly in the space provided.

Should Jake, from Document E, try to become a Superhero?
- ☐ Yes.
- ☐ No.

Explain your answer to the previous question.

_____

_____

_____

In Document E, which character tells the most lies?
- ☐ Irma
- ☐ Jake
- ☐ Robert
- ☐ Tamara

List at least three possible ways in which the Superheroes could solve the noisy key problem described in Document F. You may use ideas mentioned in the document but you must include at least one original solution.

_____

_____

_____

_____

_____

List at least two things the Superheroes in Document F could do better next time that Praxis did not mention.

_____

_____

_____

Of the characters from Documents E and F, which of them is the most athletic?
- ☐ Auslander
- ☐ Irma / Protea
- ☐ Jake
- ☐ Maya
- ☐ Moonclaw
- ☐ Praxis
- ☐ Robert / Alabaster Wight
- ☐ Tamara
- ☐ Vergiften

Explain your answer to the previous question.

_____

_____

_____

_____

RC3-990182

Form 2410-140

Please do not write in this space.

Form 2410-140

Level IV: Courage
Examination for Promotion
EXFP-LVIV

You are taking the Level IV Examination for Promotion because the Pike County Super Services Division has determined that there is a need for a Level IV Superhero. You have successfully passed the interview and you are still a potential candidate for the position.

After a brief skills review, you'll need to successfully complete three live simulation test scenarios and the Level IV Psychological Assessment in order to be promoted to Level IV.

Skills Review
Review the skills you focused on in training before continuing.

Your Level IV Superhero training focused on:

- Active neighborhoods during the night.
- Maintaining a healthy diet.
- Ranged attacks.
- The standard issue utility belt.

Scenarios
EXFP-LVIV-B

You are required to pass all three VCR (Virtual Combat Room) scenarios before moving on to the Level IV Psychological Assessment. For scenarios 10 and 12, a passing grade is 70 points. For scenario 11, a passing grade is 100 points.

Scenario 10: The Cave
Objective: Enter the cave. No points will be awarded if any one of the six senses is restricted or limited in any capacity.

Points		
	100	Cave entered within 10 seconds
	90	Cave entered within 1:00 minute
	80	Cave entered within 3:00 minutes
	70	Cave entered within 6:00 minutes

Scenario 11: Death
Objective: Remain in the VCR's Death session until you are dead. No points will be awarded for aborting the session.

Points		
	100	Death
10 bonus points awarded for each zombie permanently killed*		
*Bonus points only awarded with a successful death		

Scenario 12: The Frightening Villain
Objective: Defeat the frightening villain.

Points	100	Defeat within 2:00 minutes
	90	Defeat within 8:00 minutes
	80	Defeat within 15:00 minutes
	70	Defeat within 30:00 minutes
10 bonus points awarded for maintaining clean undergarments		

Level IV Psychological Assessment

EXFP-LVIV-C

The Level IV Psychological Assessment is given on the following pages. There is no time limit for completion of this assessment, but the length of time you take will be recorded and considered along with your responses.

Directions

Read Documents G, H, and I, and then answer the related questions. There are no right or wrong answers. A Reference Sheet has been included as an optional aid. Researching related people and events in the Hall of Humanity's archives is permitted, but will not help you.

Grading

The Super Services Division will evaluate your responses with guidance from a panel of peers at Level VII or higher. A passing grade will be acknowledged with a pay increase and official promotion to Level IV duties.

Record the date and time before you begin.

Year	Month	Day	Hour	Minute	AM/PM

Reference Sheet

Document G's narrator is Moonclaw.

In Document H, Alabaster Wight and Tamara are operating legally outside of the Pike County perimeter through the authority of a special Superhero contract.

Real Name	Superhero Name	Position
Carver	Moonclaw	Level II Superhero
Jonesy	N/A	Civilian, receptionist*
Mike	N/A	Class B villain, welder
Robert	Alabaster Wight	Level III Superhero, Superhero contractor
Tamara	Tamara	Level VI Superhero, Superhero contractor
Sallah	Sallah	Officially Recognized Superhero of Iran
Pulmo	Pulmo	Level V Superhero
Helen	N/A	Civilian, unknown
Sera	Asana	Level VII Superhero

*In Document H, Jonesy is between jobs.

Document G

The Bus Stop

Cuts on my face.

Bruises all over.

Many of them visible.

"What happened to you?" Jonesy asks.

Sweet Jonesy. I thought I'd never see him again.

I say nothing.

He stumbles back, goes for some coffee.

When I get to my desk, it happens.

Jonesy sets a mug on my desk and I notice his hoop earrings. Orange. He smiles.

The hair on my back lifts and the air suddenly smells dangerous.

I look out the window.

A bus is coming down the street.

I smell something burning.

People are crossing in front of the bus:
   a man with a stroller.
   an older woman.
   a guy in a suit on his cell phone.

A ball of fire hits the front of the bus.

I hear Jonesy inhale.

The bus driver falls forward in his seat.

The people in the office look up from their work.

I know what to do.

I jump up on my desk.

The bus swerves toward the curb.

It's not going to stop.

I leap to the file cabinets next to the window and put my fist
through the glass.

It doesn't hurt.

The man on the cell phone is on the sidewalk, now, right
in front of the bus, getting showered with the glass shards
flying away from my fist.

He doesn't have time to be surprised.

I jump out and stand in front of the bus.

I have the ability to change into a human wolf. That's one of my super powers. I can also emit a thick mist from my sweat glands that hides the transformation from others. People see my civilian form pass into a cloud, and then the cloud is so thick that they can't tell what's happening. And then out of the cloud comes a human wolf and they forget about the man that went into the cloud. I do this every time something like this happens, every time I have to change into my Superhero form right in front of people. It's a very fast process. It takes less than a second.

But today is the day I've decided to give up my secret identity. I'm going to be me, right in front of everyone, in front of Jonesy and everyone at the office, in front of everyone on the block. I don't use the mist. I don't change into the human wolf. I'm tired of the cloud.

The man on the cell phone finally sees the bus coming.

I stand between him and the bus, and I look at him for a moment and he sees me as I really am. Just a normal human being. Then he witnesses my super powers.

It doesn't hurt when the front end of the bus wraps itself around me.

My feet stay planted.

The man's cell phone slips out of his hand.

Last night, I killed a man. I killed a man who beat the crap out of me before I was able to do it. The bus slamming into me at thirty-five miles per hour doesn't hurt, but the man I fought last night was strong enough to beat me senseless. I survived by sheer luck.

The cell phone guy's arms fly up to his face.

He thinks the bus is going to run us both over but my feet stay planted.

Debris flies past me.

The cell phone hits the ground.

I feel the back of the bus tilt up for a second.

The cell phone man peeks between his arms.

The bus settles on the ground again, its inertia spent into my back.

Jonesy is staring through the office window.

He's in shock.

He doesn't know what he's seeing.

It might have been better for him if I'd have changed into the wolf.

But I'm not going to wear a disguise anymore.

The door to the bus is crushed, so I tear a hole in the side. Several people are anxious to get out. I touch them as they push past me, leaving behind a special spell that will heal their traumatized spines and organs. Then I enter the bus and start touching everyone in it. Some are unconscious. The man I saved from getting run over still hasn't even picked up his cell phone. Jonesy starts to come out of his trance.

I hop out of the bus and feel the hair rise again. A burning smell.

Jonesy is outside now, walking toward me.

I want to tell him everything.

He's ten feet away when a ball of fire hits me.

He jumps back.

The fire incinerates my clothing, roasting me naked in the street.

It hurts.

The fire is hotter than normal fire or else it wouldn't hurt at all.

I look up. A man is hovering in the sky, preparing another fire ball. I know him.

Jonesy is frantically looking around for something, blankets maybe, but the fire is almost done burning.

The man in the sky can fly and throw fire balls. He also happens to be the son of the man I killed last night. He is younger. Stronger. He is pissed.

I face him, naked, inside a ring of fire.

Document H

The Surgery

In a Deli

Jonesy was berating Robert over lunch.

Finally, Jonesy softened enough to say, "I just want you to understand — I think you are purposely falling in love with people you can never have."

Robert nodded thoughtfully.

"You may be right," he said, which was a phrase he used when he didn't agree with someone's opinion.

In a Hotel Room in Flagstaff

"I really think we should just get it over with, don't you?" Tamara hollered from the bathroom.

"Whatever you say," Robert answered. The contract job was over. His nice shirt was untucked and his dress shoes leaned against the door.

There was a sound of breaking glass.

"Oh, shit!" she cried. "I broke my pipe."

She found him on his back pretending to watch TV, trying not to pass out. There was a band-aid wrapped around the end of her pipe.

"I can still use it," she said.

She sat by the open window and started her ritual, blowing smoke out of the room every few minutes.

He flipped through the channels and stopped on the news. Apparently Sallah and Pulmo hadn't resolved the hostage crisis yet. And Kansas had lost, but he knew that already from watching the game at the brewery.

Soon the intermittent sound of the lighter ceased and Tamara flopped next to him on the bed.

"Show me some yoga," he said.

"Okay." She curled up into a ball on her back. "This one's nice."

He copied her.

"Now roll from side to side," she said.

He watched, mimicking her movements. They stopped at the same time.

She put her hand on the remote and after a while she said, "There's nothing on."

"Yeah, that's the bad thing about cable. It takes longer to decide nothing's on because you have to flip through more channels."

He closed his eyes. Gray and black swirled behind his eyelids.

Then her lips were on his and her smoky alcohol toothpaste breath touched his tongue.

And Helen (who was just a dream) and Sera Phares (who was very real, yet equally inaccessible) gently drifted away.

Helen, From the Coffee Shop

During a brief conversation with Helen in a coffee shop, Robert recorded two details:

1. She had once worked in a library.
2. She lived "practically across the street from The Grass Tree Tavern."

One month later, he realized he was in love with her. He didn't know her address, phone number, or last name, but, as she had worked in a library, he felt she would have a library card. So, instead of balancing invoices (which is what the library paid his secret identity to do), he began checking every cardholder with the first name of Helen and cross-referenced those accounts for an address within a two-block radius of The Grass Tree Tavern.

It took five months to go through every last name beginning with A, B, C, D, E, F, and G. He gave up in the middle of H, calculating that, given the high apartment turnover of the neighborhood, if she hadn't moved by now, she would have by the time he got to her name.

Despite ending his search, he thought of her constantly.

Sera Phares, From His Other Job

Robert fell in love with Sera Phares while waiting for the elevator to drop one floor. As they passed each other in the halls over the course of months, he realized she had the ability to act like everything was okay while shouldering a great amount of suffering. Of course, he couldn't be sure about that, since she never spoke about the great amounts of suffering that she obviously must be hiding.

He memorized each of her visible tattoos and even started playing guitar again. Yet, she had a boyfriend who cooked, while he could not string two sentences together in her presence.

Despite the obvious impossibility of a relationship, he thought of her constantly.

His Heart, Which Shall Hereafter Be Called "Frank"

Frank had been ripped from his body and torn into pieces. So when Robert opened his eyes in the dark hotel room, in the middle of Tamara's smoky kisses, he saw the scar on her shoulder, lit by the television, and caved.

He lost consciousness of Frank, grabbed Tamara's neck, and forced her tongue deeper into his mouth. For one second, he thought she could end it.

The Surgery

Tamara's precision was sloppy at best. Frank was not sewn together but instead crammed (still in pieces), into the gaping hole in Robert's chest, which Tamara stitched up, loosely, with dental floss.

Within two weeks his chest split open and pieces of Frank began to fall out during luncheons and block parties and bar mitzvahs.

He didn't bother to put the pieces back in.

Months later, during a library meeting on e-commerce, Robert attempted communication with himself by writing a memo.

MEMO

PRIORITY: (Low)   Medium   High

TO: You.

FROM: Me.

MESSAGE:

Though Frank is entirely missing, for one moment you felt Frank beating within you. This will be the best you can do for a long, long while.

Level IV

Psychological Assessment Questions

Form **2410-141**
RC3-990184

Name:	ID:
County: **Pike County**	Date:

How to fill out this form:
- For multiple choice questions, completely fill the box to the left of your choice.
- For write-in answers, please print legibly in the space provided.

In Document G, which of the following required the narrator to be the most courageous?
- ☐ Leaping into action before drinking his morning coffee
- ☐ Standing in front of a bus
- ☐ Giving up his secret identity
- ☐ Facing the son of the man he killed
- ☐ Acknowledging his feelings for Jonesy

If you were the narrator in Document G, what would you do first after getting hit with the fire ball?
- ☐ Stop, drop, and roll
- ☐ Call for help from other Superheroes
- ☐ Run like the wind
- ☐ Face the enemy

In Document H, why does Robert ask Tamara to show him some yoga?
- ☐ He doesn't know what else to talk about.
- ☐ He wants to learn.
- ☐ He thinks yoga will help clear his head.
- ☐ He thinks it will be hot to do yoga with her.
- ☐ He is sad.

Judging solely from the information in Document H, which of the following characters would be the most compatible partner for Robert?
- ☐ Helen
- ☐ Jonesy
- ☐ Sera Phares
- ☐ Tamara

Which of the following statements best describes Robert and Tamara's relationship in Document H?
- ☐ They are lovers.
- ☐ They are married.
- ☐ They are seeing each other.
- ☐ They are making the best of a situation.
- ☐ They don't know what they're doing.

Of the characters from Documents G and H, which of them is the most courageous?
- ☐ Carver / Moonclaw (the narrator of Document G)
- ☐ Helen
- ☐ Jonesy
- ☐ Robert
- ☐ Sera
- ☐ Tamara
- ☐ The man on the cell phone

Continued on other side

Explain your answer to the previous question.

_____

_____

_____

_____

_____

_____

Please do not write in this space.

RC3-990184

Form 2410-141

Level V: Trustworthiness
Examination for Promotion

You are taking the Level V Examination for Promotion because the Pike County Super Services Division has determined that there is a need for a Level V Superhero. You have successfully passed the interview and you are still a potential candidate for the position.

After a brief skills review, you'll need to successfully complete three live simulation test scenarios and the Level V Psychological Assessment in order to be promoted to Level V.

Skills Review
Review the skills you focused on in training before continuing.

Your Level V Superhero training focused on:

- Dangerous neighborhoods during the day.
- Team fighting.
- Anger management.
- The Super Driving Test for Pike County-Approved Super Vehicles

Scenarios

You are required to pass all three VCR (Virtual Combat Room) scenarios before moving on to the Level V Psychological Assessment. For each scenario, a passing grade is 70 points.

Scenario 13: The Dream World
Objective: Spend time in the Dream World scenario without accepting gifts, stealing, playing games, ingesting food or beverage, self-administering drugs, engaging in sexually stimulating activity, petting animals, or spending any of the one million dollars you start the scenario with.

Points		
	100	Objectives met for 48 consecutive hours (water permitted)
	90	Objectives met for 36 consecutive hours (water permitted)
	80	Objectives met for 30 consecutive hours
	70	Objectives met for 24 consecutive hours
10 bonus points awarded for not sleeping		
20 bonus points awarded for having absolutely no fun		

Scenario 14: The Clock

Objective: Work the day shift at a mining plant for six months. Virtual time accelerators will be employed so that this simulation will take fewer than eight days. It is recommended that you abstain from drinking fluids for 24 hours before this VCR session.

Points		
	100	Never late, 8 hours of actual work logged each day
	85	Late fewer than 3 times, 8 hours of actual work logged each day
	70	Late fewer than 6 times, 8 hours of actual work logged each day
10 bonus points awarded for consistent, quality work		
-10 points for each total hour of accumulated late time		

Scenario 15: The Charismatic Villain

Objective: Spend four hours with the villain without becoming convinced that the VCR is the real world and the world outside of it is just a simulation. No points will be awarded if the villain is rendered unconscious or dead.

Points		
	100	Belief in real world maintained while fully engaged in conversation
	85	Belief in real world maintained with limited conversation
	70	Belief in real world maintained without talking
10 bonus points awarded for being polite		
-50 points for plugging ears or fabricating other means of not hearing the villain		

Level V Psychological Assessment

EXFP-LVV-C

The Level V Psychological Assessment is given on the following pages. There is no time limit for completion of this assessment, but the length of time you take will be recorded and considered along with your responses.

Directions

Read Documents I, J, and K, and then answer the related questions. There are no right or wrong answers. A Reference Sheet has been included as an optional aid. Researching related people and events in the Hall of Humanity's archives is permitted, but may or may not help you.

Grading

The Super Services Division will evaluate your responses with guidance from a panel of peers at Level VIII or higher. A passing grade will be acknowledged with a pay increase and official promotion to Level V duties.

Record the date and time before you begin.

Year	Month	Day	Hour	Minute	AM/PM

Reference Sheet
EXFP-LVV-D

In Document K, Auslander, Sera, and Edward are operating legally outside of the Pike County perimeter through the authority of a special Superhero contract.

Real Name	Superhero Name	Position
Auslander	Auslander	Level VII Superhero
Sera	Asana	Level VII Superhero
Garrote	Garrote	Level V Superhero
Edward	Edward	Level IV Superhero
Luca	Luca	Level VIII Pilot

Document I

The Apartment

Auslander found Asana kneeling beside Garrote. She moved her hands in the air above him as color returned to Garrote's pale face.

"What happened?" Auslander said.

"That beam collapsed on his head. Fortunately, he has a thick skull."

Garrote's eyes opened. He grabbed Asana's shoulders.

"Thank you," he said. "I needed that. You're always taking care of me."

"You're always taking care of me," Asana said.

Garrote took a deep breath. He looked around. "I think I'm okay."

"Is everyone out of the building?" Asana asked Auslander.

"Yep. Everything's under control."

"Don't you live around here?"

Auslander nodded.

"Is your apartment okay?" Asana asked.

"I kind of want to check."

Garrote stood up. "We'll go with you."

"You're still healing," Asana said.

"It's okay. I'm ready to die all over again."

Auslander quizzed Asana as they walked.

"How is the counseling going?" he said.

"Fine," Asana said. "Actually, really good."

She looked him in the eye when she said that.

"And how are things with the boyfriend?"

"Edward is amazing. I found another amazing person. It doesn't seem fair."

"Well, if it's not fair, then it's probably real. Good for you, Asana."

Garrote said, "Even I like Edward. Those two are good."

Auslander flipped through his keys.

"It was such a mild earthquake," he said. "I don't expect there to be much damage, but...you never know."

He unlocked the door.

They walked in carefully, stepping over piles of old paperback novels.

"Holy wow, Auslander," Asana said. "I'm so sorry."

Auslander looked around. "Oh. No, that's pretty much like it always is."

Garrote pushed past them and headed toward the kitchen. "Got anything to drink?"

Auslander shrugged. "Help yourself."

"Whoah," Garrote said.

"What?" Asana asked.

"I don't think this is normal," Garrote called from the next room.

Auslander and Asana joined him in the kitchen. A massive slab of rock had shoved its way up through the floor of the basement apartment. Loose checkered floor tiles covered the floor.

"That's funny. I usually keep the rock slab in the closet," Auslander said.

Garrote looked closer. "That's not even the weirdest thing."

He blew dust off the side of the rock. "There's writing on it," he said.

"What is it?" Asana asked.

"Very old Greek," Garrote said, moving his fingers over it.

"Can you read it?" Auslander asked.

"Yeah. Give me a minute. Somebody carved this a long time ago. Wait. Auslander—it mentions you by name."

Document J

Message from Apostolos
Loosely translated by Garrote

Dear Auslander,

    I'm your best friend from a time that doesn't exist anymore. In that time I was a time-traveling Superhero at Pike County Super Services Division. You trained me and we became great friends. But then the world was destroyed. I went back in time to try to save it, but no matter what I tried, nothing worked. Often, I only made matters worse. In fact, the only thing that kept the planet from being destroyed was when I avoided that time period altogether.

    Of course, I don't know any of this first-hand. This is what was related to me from a future version of myself. He truly, truly cherished your friendship, but there was no possible way for him to live in your time without indirectly destroying the planet. He was the butterfly that flapped its wings and no matter which way he flapped them, the world kept blowing up.

    My future self told me what I had to do: leave my time period during my adolescence and never return. So here I am, 1600 years or so before your time, chiseling this letter on a slab of rock that is going to protrude through your basement apartment during the mostly mild earthquake of ███. This wasn't too hard to orchestrate, since a different future version of myself provided me with copies of files from the Hall of Humanity's archives which described the exact location of this stone. Don't worry—another future version of me verified that things were still okay (the planet did not blow up from me contacting you).

    You'd think time travel would be a pretty cool power to have, but it's not. Most of the time, you're told what to do by various versions of yourself who are from some future time in which you've really messed things up. Of course, you could ignore their advice and just do what you want, but come on—if you can't trust your future self, who can you trust?

So, what I want to say, really, is that things will be fine and the world won't blow up (my future selves have confirmed this), if you do what I say, which is why I'm contacting you. Here's the deal: do not go on the contract job to Diamond City. Bad things will happen if you do.

Of course, I know what you're thinking. You're thinking, how do I know this isn't an enemy's message cleverly disguised as coming from a friend? And I know you'll consider that I know that you know that I know what you'll end up doing. So let me reassure you that whatever I tell you in this message is the right thing to tell you for you to do what you need to do, which may or may not be what I've suggested. You always were an independent thinker, an outsider, according to my future self that knew you. I know you'll weigh the options and make the right choice. I know this, because I snuck a peek at the future, and all is well, or at least as well as I and several thousand future selves could figure out how to make it. I'm sorry for any inconvenience you may experience, but many future selves have assured me that your devotion to your Superhero duties is something you place above all, so it is with only a little guilt that I willingly manipulate your future. It's for the greater good.

Your friend,

Apostolos

P.S. I can't tell you my real name, because that ends up blowing up the planet. Sorry.

Document K

The Walk

I woke up. Water was dripping on my face. I thought the tent was leaking, but when I opened my eyes I saw Sera leaning over me.

"Auslander."

(That was all she said.)

Edward was dying at the bottom of the canyon. Or maybe he was finished by now, I didn't know.

(He was Sera's Edward.)

Three thousand gallons of poison were drifting down the river and would soon enter Diamond City's water supply.

(There was no way to warn them.)

Our radio was gone, and we had no way to travel except walk.

(And my leg had been shot.)

Luca was supposed to take us back, but her chopper was hurtling out of control when we last saw it. It disappeared behind a peak just before we heard an explosion.

(I am assuming Luca is dead.)

And now Sera was leaning over me, dripping warm tears on my face.

We were at least three days from the highway with no food or water. Sera's healing powers had disappeared when we first hiked into the area, so instead she fashioned a splint for my leg while I injected myself with drugs.

(It made me dizzy, but it took away the pain.)

When we were ambushed back in the canyon, Sera, knowing that Edward was going to die, hauled me out instead. She duct taped the medical kit to my leg, strapped me to her back somehow, and climbed up the steep canyon face as quickly as possible.

(Sera is incredibly strong.)

I hoped we had enough drugs to get me to the highway. Reuben would eventually send a unit after us, but we couldn't wait.

(We were being followed.)

Moisture trickled off wind-blown branches.

(It kept us cool.)

It was all I could do just to walk on my right leg, even with the splint and the drugs. Sera walked ahead of me, taking us on a direct path to the highway.

(She knew they were close behind.)

We stopped to rest at the top of an incline.

"Do you think Luca bailed somehow?" Sera asked. She didn't look at me.

"No," I answered, out of breath. I didn't have the energy to sugar coat it.

She nodded.

(She didn't ask about Edward.)

We walked up and down gradual slopes while the sun dried our clothes. At the top of a range, Sera took a look around before leading us down through a seasonal flood prairie. It was a good place for an ambush, but I didn't need to point this out.

(She had decided to cut through to save time.)

Prairie grass brushed my chin as we descended into the valley. Suddenly, Sera turned and jerked me into the grass.

"I think I made a mistake," she whispered.

My stomach knotted as she started pulling guns out of holsters: one from behind her back, one off of her hip, and a third from her right ankle. She let the rifle fall off her shoulder. All the guns went to the ground except her favorite semi-automatic. I stayed crouched, my leg straight out in the splint, trying to steady my gun hand.

(I wondered how many there were and what kind of a chance we had.)

Sera scanned the trees, taking stock of possible hiding places. I tried to help, but the drugs kept me from concentrating. Suddenly Sera raised her gun and fired.

(Through the grass I saw a man stagger and fall.)

Sera began pumping bullets into the surrounding woods. She emerged out of the grass and shot two or three times, then ducked and rolled, popping up in a new spot, firing. Then she flew past, grabbing a gun on the way and leaving an empty one behind. Their plan had been to mow us down as we walked through the prairie bed, but Sera's instincts saved us.

(They couldn't see us unless we sat up to take a shot.)

I tried to tag one of them but after firing two bullets way off the mark, I decided to stay low and reload for Sera.

(The drugs were affecting my aim.)

She was brilliant. Every time one of them shot at us, she was able to pinpoint their location. She didn't have to wait for them to peek out from behind the trees. Our bullets could go through Kevlar, so she shot right through the trees and whatever else got in the way. When the shooting stopped, we sat still for a minute.

(My breathing was loud.)

Two shots whispered through the grass in front of my face. Sera jumped up and fired three times, then crouched.

(She didn't seem to breathe at all.)

After a few minutes, we collected the guns and crawled to the edge of the clearing. Sera used the scope to scan the opposite side of the field.

(I gave myself another shot in the leg before we started hiking.)

I used the last of the drugs just before sunset. By the time it got dark, I was struggling to keep up.

Sera slowed down.

> (She thought I wouldn't notice.)

"Sera, I—"

She stopped and looked at me.

> (I couldn't see her face in the dark but I knew it was hard and unrelenting.)

I tried to say it, but I couldn't with her looking at me. So we hiked on.

The moon was out when I collapsed an hour later. I tried to get up, but I didn't want to badly enough. Sera came over to help, but I knew I could say it now.

"I'm done."

She stood over me and stared.

> (Edward and Luca were dead. The entire population of Diamond City was probably poisoned by now.)

"Go on," I said. "You can find me by chopper."

"You'll be dead. But I will come get you. I'll bring a Level X with me and we'll clean this place out. Reuben was a fool to put us in this mess."

"Will you talk to my family?" I asked.

She nodded.

> (I tried to think of what I wanted her to say.)

"I know," she said.

My vision blurred.

"Sera?"

She looked at me.

"I'm sorry," I said.

She shrugged. "We tried."

"We failed."

Sera crouched in front of me.

"You're right," she said. "We lost."

"You better get going," I said.

"You know I'd carry you."

"And you know that then we'd both die. I'm out of drugs. My leg is busted. I'm finished. You need to get out of here."

She stood and backed away. We looked at each other. I tried to tell her with my eyes to just go.

(It was getting harder by the second.)

Just go, I said to her in my head.

Just go.

Then she left, silently disappearing at a run.

I dragged myself over to a tree and slept.

When I woke up it was light out and I didn't feel so miserable. I thought of my family and smiled. I felt sorry for failing, but now I could feel good that I had tried. I hoped Sera would make it out okay.

A lemming scurried through the weeds in front of me. I could smell the faint scent of smoke, of something burning. The air on my skin felt cool and fresh.

Level V

Psychological Assessment Questions

Form **2410-142**
RC3-990186

Name:	ID:
County: **Pike County**	Date:

How to fill out this form:
- For multiple choice questions, completely fill the box to the left of your choice.
- For write-in answers, please print legibly in the space provided.

In Document I, what is the primary reason why Asana is going to counseling?

- ☐ Counseling is a normal part of living a healthy, positive life.
- ☐ She uses counseling to help deal with a loved one's death.
- ☐ She wishes to become less sensitive toward others.
- ☐ She has a debilitating anxiety caused by a fear of wheat.
- ☐ There is not enough information to figure it out.
- ☐ Other:

_____

_____

Based on the information in Documents I, J, and K, should Auslander have gone on the contract job partially chronicled in Document K?

- ☐ Yes.
- ☐ No.

Explain your answer to the previous question.

_____

_____

_____

Does Document J foretell what happens to Auslander in Document K?

- ☐ Yes.
- ☐ No.
- ☐ When time travel is involved, foretelling is just a matter of perception.
- ☐ There is not enough information to figure it out.

At the very end of Document K, what do you think Auslander smelled that was burning?

_____

_____

Why do you think Garrote, from Document I, was not there to help Asana in Document K?

- ☐ Garrote can't be everywhere at all times.
- ☐ Garrote refuses to work contract jobs for Reuben.
- ☐ Asana told Garrote not to go on the mission.
- ☐ Garrote is not reliable.
- ☐ Garrote is not a licensed contractor.
- ☐ Garrote knew that the mission was going to fail and didn't want to be there.

Of the characters from Documents I, J, and K, which of them is the most trustworthy?

- ☐ Apostolos
- ☐ Asana
- ☐ Auslander
- ☐ Edward
- ☐ Garrote
- ☐ Luca
- ☐ Reuben

Explain your answer to the previous question.

_____

_____

_____

Please do not write in this space.

Level VI: Vigilance
Examination for Promotion

EXFP-LVVI

Pike County Super Services Div.

You are taking the Level VI Examination for Promotion because the Pike County Super Services Division has determined that there is a need for a Level VI Superhero. You have successfully passed the interview and you are still a potential candidate for the position.

After a brief skills review, you'll need to successfully complete three live simulation test scenarios and the Level VI Psychological Assessment in order to be promoted to Level VI.

Skills Review
Review the skills you focused on in training before continuing.

Your Level VI Superhero training focused on:

- Dangerous neighborhoods during the night.
- Villain encounters of unlimited duration.
- How to tell if someone's lying.
- Yoga.

Scenarios

You are required to pass all three VCR (Virtual Combat Room) scenarios before moving on to the Level VI Psychological Assessment. For each scenario, a passing grade is 70 points.

Scenario 16: The Neighborhood Watch
Objective: Keep watch over the neighborhood from the living room of a household for one night. Notify the police of suspicious activity. Responding to emergencies does not penalize you, but doesn't earn points and is not recommended. This scenario only requires you to keep watch.

Points		
	100	100% of suspicious activity reported
	85	98% of suspicious activity reported
	70	96% of suspicious activity reported
10 bonus points awarded for not leaving the living room		

Scenario 17: The Babysitting Job
Objective: Maintain an 8-year-old child's personal health and safety for four hours. The child has dust, peanut, and pollen allergies and has a fear of electronic devices.

Points		
	100	Health and safety maintained, no incidents
	90	Health and safety maintained, no serious incidents
	80	Health and safety maintained, no injuries or near-death experiences
	70	Health and safety maintained, incidents resolved but some minor healing required for full restoration of health
20 bonus points awarded for not using any super powers		

Scenario 18: The Tricky Villain

Objective: Transport the villain from a holding cell to a special containment room in the state penitentiary.

Points		
	100	Villain transported without incident
	90	Villain transported, some scuffles but no serious incidents
	80	Villain transported, serious incidents resolved without critical injury
	70	Villain transported
	10 bonus points awarded for never blinking	

Level VI Psychological Assessment

EXFP-LVVI-C

The Level VI Psychological Assessment is given on the
following pages. There is no time limit for completion of this
assessment, but the length of time you take will be recorded
and considered along with your responses.

Directions

Read Documents L and M, and then answer the related
questions. There are no right or wrong answers. A Reference
Sheet has been included as an optional aid. Researching
related people and events in the Hall of Humanity's archives
is permitted, but may or may not help you. Reviewing the
Level V Psychological Assessment documents is encouraged
and may help you, but is not required for passing.

Grading

The Super Services Division will evaluate your responses
with guidance from a panel of peers at Level IX or higher.
A passing grade will be acknowledged with a pay increase
and official promotion to Level VI duties.

Record the date and time before you begin.

Year	Month	Day	Hour	Minute	AM/PM

Reference Sheet
EXFP-LVVI-D

Document L takes place one day after the events of
Document K. Garrote was the first Superhero to arrive at
Asana's location, and escorted her home. Special Superhero
contracts were issued for Carver, Praxis, Pulmo, and Sallah
authorizing the capture of the villains responsible for the
poisoning of Diamond City. The contract was carried out in
good faith.

Real Name	Superhero Name	Position
Garrote	Garrote	Level V Superhero
Sera	Asana	Level VII Superhero
Robert	Alabaster Wight	Level V Superhero
Maya	N/A	Level IV Administrative Assistant (half-time)
Mattie	N/A	Civilian, student
Trapper	Trapper	Level VI Superhero
Unknown	N/A	Civilian, concession stand operator

Document L

Pike County Telegram
Services transmits and
delivers messages by
telegram subject to the
terms and conditions
printed on the reverse side
of this form.

Pike County Telegram Services

TELEGRAM

A Division of Pike County Tele-Services

Office use only

PH - High priority
PA - Average priority
PL - Low priority
OB - Obsolete message
DE - Disregard entirely

RIDING THE CHOPPER HOME STOP GARROTE SAYS I GOT
A JOKE STOP SERA SAYS I'M NOT IN THE MOOD STOP
GARROTE SAYS IT'S OKAY IT'S A GOOD ONE STOP SERA
SAYS NOTHING STOP GARROTE SAYS WHY DOES REUBEN
WEAR LONG COATS STOP SERA SAYS I DON'T KNOW STOP
GARROTE SAYS TO MAKE HIM LOOK LIKE HE'S NOT
ABOUT TO PULL OUT A GUN AND SHOOT EVERYBODY STOP
SERA SAYS THAT DOESN'T MAKE ANY SENSE STOP
GARROTE SAYS THAT'S THE POINT IT DOESN'T MAKE
SENSE THAT'S WHY HE DOES IT FULL STOP

Document M

A Superhero Romance

SPOTLIGHT ON: Alabaster Wight!
Civilian Name: Robert Good
Position: Level V Superhero
Eye Color: Hazel
Favorite Food: Pasta
Favorite Color: Chartreuse
Lucky Number: 7
Discovered Super Powers at: Age 15
Hobbies: Backpacking, reading, and
volunteering at the local public library

Robert and Maya worked at the Hall of Humanity. Maya worked as a half-time Level IV Administrative Assistant ($14.59 per hour), and Robert worked as a Level V Superhero ($42,396 per year).

They once had this conversation while passing each other in the hall:

ROBERT: Hi.
MAYA: Hi.

After that, Robert began finding reasons to look over files kept remarkably near Maya's desk. Periodically, they even talked. Finally, when Robert discovered *The Communist Manifesto* on Maya's desk, they started a weeks-long discussion on utopian government.

However, weeks were all they had, as soon Maya found a job as a paralegal across town and turned in her two weeks notice.

For Maya's last day, they agreed to get ice cream after work, but as Robert was pulling 17 people from a flaming, overturned railcar, the weather turned cold. While changing into civilian clothes, he prepared himself for disappointment, as he didn't expect Maya to want ice cream on such a cold day. But at five o'clock, he found Maya waiting outside the Hall of Humanity, sitting on the gaudy sculpture that allegedly represented justice.

"It got cold," he said. "I thought you wouldn't show."

She smiled. "Ice cream is best on a cold day."

They argued about ice cream and cold weather and Marxism all the way to the ice cream shop. As they ate, the conversation turned from Marxism to politics to politics-at-work and somehow back to ice cream after discussing regional differences in the number of people that fall off of tall buildings. Then, the conversation shifted back to Marxism once more.

After ice cream, Robert walked Maya to her bus stop. Before boarding the bus, she stared at him for a second.

"Call me at work sometime," he said. "We'll get ice cream again."

She nodded.

Then the bus carried her away and Robert started to walk home. Along the way, he made up a story in his head involving Maya getting off the bus and following him, trying to catch up— following him because she was filled with the same fanatical joy that he was.

SUPERHERO FUN FACT!
Despite their tendency toward stoicism, Superheroes are capable of feeling a wide range of emotions—just like normal human beings!

He thought that maybe after he got home, took off his shoes, and put on some music, she would knock on the door and declare her love for him.

The stars were dim that night.

Were there a villain capable of holding a Superhero's tongue hostage whenever the hero was inclined to pursue romantic intentions, it is possible that Robert's closed-mouth approach toward potential mates would be blamed on this villain. However, no such villain has ever surfaced, so it is reasonable to assume that Robert was the way he was because of his own ineptitude.

This inability to engage people romantically was demonstrated one evening at a coffee shop, six months after Maya quit her job at the Hall of Humanity. Robert was reading and enjoying his night off when a woman asked him what time it was.

Minutes later, she bothered him again to ask what he was reading. Eventually, she sucked him into discussing neuropsychology, her major. Or at least, at first glance it may have looked as though a discussion were taking place, though in reality, she did all of the talking while Robert tried to nod in ways that made him look intelligent.

SUPERHERO FUN FACT!
The majority of Superheroes have no particular weakness outside of what harms most humans. If something seems dangerous or harmful to you, most likely it will have a negative impact on your local Superhero, too.

To Robert, someone that was willing to talk to him while he was dressed in civilian clothes was most welcome, and because of this, he moved to her table and listened to her speak about neuropsychology until the coffee shop closed.

Outside, before parting, Robert said, "Well, Mattie, it was nice meeting you."

The coffee shop door locked behind them.

"Yes, nice talking to you," Mattie said.

She blinked.

"Have a good night," he said.

"You too."

They parted. Robert started the walk to his apartment thinking about what a good thing it was that he didn't get her number. After all, he was rather bored with neuropsychology these days.

Moments later, he wished he had gotten her number because at least they might have become friends. But it was too late—he hadn't gotten it and now she was gone.

Desperately, Robert pivoted and looked, hoping that maybe she had followed him, that maybe she wanted to chat some more over a late night tea at his apartment. But she was nowhere to be seen.

At home, while he sipped a cup of Earl Grey, he glanced often at the door.

Outside, the last snow of the year began to fall.

On a particularly cool evening that summer, Robert continued his civilian life by seeing the usual summer action flick with the usual movie-going pal, Trapper (A.K.A. the Psi-Clone, Level VI Superhero, $46,454 per year). Trapper worked with Robert at the Hall of Humanity.

SUPERHERO FUN FACT! Superheroes are not immune from depression and other forms of mental illness. It's possible for a Superhero to suffer from all kinds of mental maladies—even schizophrenia. However, with treatment and a strong support group, Superheroes affected by mental illness can go on to lead productive Superhero lives.

Trapper was oblivious to a lot of things, and on this night that included being oblivious to the rare grace of the woman behind the concession counter. Her beauty defied the bland uniform on her body, which prompted Robert to choose her line even though it was longer.

Trapper didn't notice. He was too busy talking about the Beatles. Just as Mattie had enjoyed talking about neuropsychology, Trapper never stopped talking about iconic rock.

Robert was doing his best to act like he wasn't paying attention when Trapper said, "So I was like, 'Ban the Beatles! What are you, Communist?!' I can't support those Russian ideas, man. Look what Communism did to their country!"

Without taking his eyes off of the woman behind the counter, Robert said, "The U.S.S.R was Socialist at best, not Communist. And Marx and Engels weren't Russian."

Trapper ignored him. "So I turned him over to the coppers and I said, 'Shouldn't have robbed a liquor store with a patriotic Superhero around.' He went easy."

"Small Super Cola," Robert said.

SUPERHERO FUN FACT!
In today's dangerous world, a Superhero needs even more than super powers to do well. That's why most Superheroes use skills and abilities they've developed through extensive training. Your local Superhero could be trained in a variety of things, from jujitsu to yoga, from computer programming to Chinese!

The woman behind the counter nodded and artfully dropped a cup under the nozzle. As the cup filled, her fingers punched keys on the cash register.

"Three seventy-five," she said, smiling. She instinctively knew that he didn't want anything else with that.

She took his five-dollar bill and gracefully placed money in his hand, saying, "One twenty-five is your change. Enjoy the show."

"Thank you," Robert said.

When the movie got out, Robert saw her locking up the cash registers. Droves of people divided them, so he simply watched her through the crowd as he and Trapper walked by.

"You need a lift?" Trapper asked. "I've got the spinner tonight."

"No, thanks. I feel like walking."

"Suit yourself. Take it easy."

"Yeah. See ya'."

Robert took giant breaths of fresh air as he walked home. Thoughts of spending the night in his empty apartment mellowed him. Several times he looked back to see if anyone was following, but the trees and bushes didn't even move in the wind.

When he got home, he slumped to the floor to take off his shoes. Sighing, he leaned against the wall.

There was a knock.

He got up and tentatively opened the door. A figure stepped out of the darkness.

"Maya?" he said.

"I—I followed you home."

"You were at the movie?"

"—Ten months ago," she finished.

He thought for a moment and started to frown, but she grabbed him and held him and tears traveled from her cheek to his. His frown disappeared. Their mouths connected and their chests pounded against each other. Then, twirling round, they left the world behind for one brief and simple period of eternity. And that's hard to do, even for a Superhero.

"A Superhero Romance" first appeared in *Superhero Lit*, Volume 30, No. 5.

Level VI

Form **2410-143**
RC3-990188

Name:	ID:
County: **Pike County**	Date:

How to fill out this form:
- For multiple choice questions, completely fill the box to the left of your choice.
- For write-in answers, please print legibly in the space provided.

Write a short paragraph about Garrote's joke from Document L. Focus the paragraph on whether or not Garrote's joke made sense.

_____

_____

_____

_____

During or after reading Document L, did you laugh?
- ☐ Yes.
- ☐ No.
- ☐ I'm not sure.

In Document M, why did Maya wait ten months to approach Robert after following him home?
- ☐ She was waiting to see how another romantic situation would turn out, first.
- ☐ She is naturally shy about relationships.
- ☐ She was apprehensive about becoming romantically involved with a Superhero.
- ☐ Other:

_____

If you were Robert, from Document M, which of the following characters would you be most interested in dating?
- ☐ Mattie
- ☐ Maya
- ☐ The woman behind the counter

Explain your answer to the previous question.

_____

_____

Of the characters from Documents L and M, which of them is the most vigilant?
- ☐ Garrote
- ☐ Mattie
- ☐ Maya
- ☐ Reuben
- ☐ Robert / Alabaster Wight
- ☐ Sera
- ☐ The woman behind the counter
- ☐ Trapper / the Psi-Clone

Explain your answer to the previous question.

_____

_____

_____

RC3-990188

Form 2410-143

Continued on other side

Please do not write in this space.

Level VII: Virtue
Examination for Promotion

Pike County Super Services Div.

You are taking the Level VII Examination for Promotion because the Pike County Super Services Division has determined that there is a need for a Level VII Superhero. You have successfully passed the interview and you are still a potential candidate for the position.

After a brief skills review, you'll need to successfully complete three live simulation test scenarios and the Level VII Psychological Assessment in order to be promoted to Level VII.

Skills Review
Review the skills you focused on in training before continuing.

Your Level VII Superhero training focused on:

- Flying villains.
- Storming villain lairs.
- Tricks and traps.
- Battle-related physics.

Scenarios
EXFP-LVVII-B

You are required to pass all three VCR (Virtual Combat Room) scenarios before moving on to the Level VII Psychological Assessment. For each scenario, a passing grade is 70 points.

Scenario 19: Volunteer Experience
Objective: Construct a well near a small desert village.

Points		
	100	Well constructed within 4 hours
	90	Well constructed within 1 day
	80	Well constructed within 3 days
	70	Well constructed within 7 days
10 bonus points awarded for quality work		
10 bonus points awarded for not eating the village's food		
-5 points for each self-vocalized complaint		

Scenario 20: The Smelly Homeless Person
Objective: Invite the homeless person into your home, and then do the following in this order:
1. Cook the homeless person a meal.
2. Arrange bedding and a pillow for a night's stay in the guest room.
3. Sleep in the adjacent room to the homeless person with the door open.
4. Provide a hot shower, washrag, soap, shampoo, conditioner, and a towel.
5. Clean the bedding, bathroom, and kitchen.

	100	Objectives met, compliments earned on steps 1 through 4
Points	93	Objectives met, some compliments earned from the guest
	86	Objectives met, no compliments earned from the guest
	78	Objectives met, fewer than six complaints from the guest
	70	Objectives met
10 bonus points awarded for not retching		
10 bonus points awarded for not using any super powers		

Scenario 21: The Villain You Love

Objective: Render the villain unconscious. No points will be awarded if the villain is killed or mortally wounded.

	100	The villain is unconscious within 2:00 minutes
Points	90	The villain is unconscious within 6:00 minutes
	80	The villain is unconscious within 12:00 minutes
	70	The villain is unconscious within 18:00 minutes
10 bonus points awarded for tricking the villain into thinking you're going bad for them		
-5 points for calling the villain an endearing term		

Level VII Psychological Assessment

EXFP-LVVII-C

The Level VII Psychological Assessment is given on the following pages. There is no time limit for completion of this assessment, but the length of time you take will be recorded and considered along with your responses.

Directions

Read Documents N and O, and then answer the related questions. There are no right or wrong answers. A Reference Sheet has been included as an optional aid. Researching related people and events in the Hall of Humanity's archives is permitted, and will most likely help you. Writing on Document O is permitted.

Grading

The Super Services Division will evaluate your responses with guidance from a panel of peers at Level IX or higher. A passing grade will be acknowledged with a pay increase and official promotion to Level VII duties.

Record the date and time before you begin.

Year	Month	Day	Hour	Minute	AM/PM

Reference Sheet
EXFP-LVVII-D

Document N is an excerpt from the journal of Alabaster Wight.

Real Name	Superhero Name	Position
Robert	Alabaster Wight	Level V Superhero
Pulmo	Pulmo	Level VIII Superhero
Maya	N/A	Civilian, paralegal
Jerboa	Jerboa	Level I Superhero*
Auslander	Auslander	Deceased

*When Document O was written, Jerboa was a Level II Superhero.

Document N

Shit. My hair's a mess.

Pulmo has spotted me. I'm asking
for it. I haven't gone home yet,
just sitting here next to my locker,
writing.

He says:
you look like you need a day off.

I say:
That's because I do.

call in sick tomorrow.

I can't.

I'd call in sick once in awhile, but everyone knows I have a natural resistance to all earthborn diseases. you're lucky.

Because I can get sick?

Because you're human.

I don't feel very. human.

Trust me, you're human.

He leaves the locker room laughing.

an

I'm home now.

I'll tell you a secret:

I've become stupid from the drinking.

And I'm the only
one who can tell.

I know superheroes aren't supposed to
drink so much, but lately that's the
only way I can get out of the costume.
After 3 glasses of scotch, the old
jazz songs sound good again and I
start not caring, even if it's just for a
morning. Then I sleep the daylight away,
get dressed, and enter the night ~~away~~ again.

an

Maya broke up with me already. It's kind
of a relief, actually. I knew they'd find
out at work that we were dating,
and I was dreading a conversation
that would have gone like this:

Someone says:

Are you dating Maya?

I say:
Yep. I'm dating
Maya.

You?

Um...
(Try to act like
they didn't just
imply I was a
loser.)

I mean, you know...
err, Congratulations, Al!

Thanks.
(Turn my lower
lip to stone so
it doesn't hurt
when I bite it.)

an

Patrolling with Jerboa is getting awkward. I suggested she round out her experience by training under one of the others, but she's too picky. She doesn't approve of Garrote's methods. She thinks (and she's probably right) that Fulmo wants to get in her pants. And Asana has too many problems of her own to take on a trainee.

Jerboa's abilities only complicate the situation. Her instincts are good, and she's learned quite a bit in a short amount of time. It's difficult for us to find a tough fight. We'll both have plenty of good scraps when we switch to solo patrols, but until then there may not be anything in this city to challenge us. I think this might be giving her a warped sense of reality.

It's to be expected. She's much better than me, and because of that she won't learn as quickly. I learned when I was still training under Auslander. His archenemy, Vergiften, caught me in the throat with a poison dart. Auslander was doing all he could just to keep himself alive, so I had 30 seconds to solve the problem or I was dead. Auslander couldn't help me. I was alone.

Jerboa has no clue that if we were in a tough fight and I had to make a choice between rescuing a civilian or saving her, I would sell her out in a second. She would be on her own, like I was with the poison. It wasn't until I had 30 seconds to live that I realized what superheroes were up against, what we were really fighting.

My phone is ringing.

Document O

The Weekly Double Word Find
This week's Double Word Find comes from **Jerboa**, Level II Superhero at Pike County Super Services Division!

Socially Responsible Video Game Review Part 1

```
T H E G A M E I S C A L L E D A N
T I-T E R R O R I S T B O M B S Q
U A D.Y O U M I G H T T H I N K T
H E M A I N O B J E C T I V E O F
T H I S G A M E I S T O D I S M A
N T L E B O M B S P L A N T E D B
Y E T E R R O R I S T S.N O P E!T H
E T E R R O R I S T S H A V E T A
K E N O V E R V A R I O U S E N A V
I R O N M E N T S(R A N G I N G F
R O M A N A I R P L A N E T O T H
E M O U N T R U S H M O R E N A T
I O N A L M E M O R I A L)A N D Y F
O U R J O B A S A M E M B E R O F B
T H E A N T I-T E R R O R I S T B
O M B S Q U A D I S T O P L A N T
B O M B S Y O U R S E L F I N O R
D E R T O D E S T R O Y T H E T R
R R O R I S T S.O N C E Y O U R O
O M B S A R E S E T,R U S H T O D
S A F E D I S T A N C E T O D E T
O N A T E T H E M A N D W A T C H
A M O V I E C L I P O F T H E T E
R R O R I S T S G E T T I N G B L
```

Socially Responsible Video Game Review Part 2

```
O W N U P.A N T I-T E R R O R I S
T B O M B S Q U A D I S H I G H L
Y E N T E R T A I N I N G T O P L
A Y,B U T I T F A I L S M I S E R
A B L Y A S A S O C I A L L Y R A
S P O N S I B L E V I D E O G A M
E.Y O U C A N S A V E H O S T A G
E S I F Y O U W A N T B U T T Y O
A R E N'T P P E N A L I Z E D I F
H E Y W I N D U P B E I N G C O Y
L A T E R A L D A M A G E.I F O B
U R E F U S E T O U S E G B O M B
A N D T R Y T O S H O O T A L L S
F T H E T E R R O R I S T S I N J
T E A D,T H E G A M E W I L L J E
S T G E N E R A T S A N D T H E L E V
R O R I S T S A N D E R E N D.T H I
L W I L L N E S N O O T H E R O P T
L E A V E S N O O T H E R O P T A T
O N B U T T O B L O W U P W H A T E
V E R I T I S T H A V E T T A K E N
R R O R I S T S S H A V E T T A K E N
O V E R,T H U S D O I N G T H E
R D I R T Y W O R K F O R T H E M.
```

Level VII

Psychological Assessment Questions

Form **2410-144**
RC3-990190

Name:	ID:
County: **Pike County**	Date:

How to fill out this form:
- For multiple choice questions, completely fill the box to the left of your choice.
- For write-in answers, please print legibly in the space provided.

In Document N, Alabaster Wight writes, "It wasn't until I had thirty seconds to live that I realized what Superheroes were up against, what we were really fighting." What does he believe Superheroes are really fighting?

_____

_____

_____

_____

_____

Why can't Alabaster Wight, from Document N, call in sick?
- ☐ Alabaster Wight doesn't get sick.
- ☐ Alabaster Wight feels obligated to work.
- ☐ Alabaster Wight is out of sick leave hours.
- ☐ Alabaster Wight's therapist has encouraged him to work regularly.
- ☐ Alabaster Wight is trying hard for a promotion.
- ☐ There is not enough information to figure it out.

In Document O, why did Jerboa choose to write her commentary on a video game in the form of a word find puzzle?
- ☐ Jerboa doesn't want people to read it.
- ☐ Jerboa likes word find puzzles.
- ☐ Jerboa is making a statement.
- ☐ Jerboa felt it would have a better chance of being published.

In Document O, how many words can you find?

_____

In Document O, of the words you found, how many do you consider inappropriate for use in a professional setting?

_____

In Document O, is it possible to find the word IRAQ?
- ☐ Yes.
- ☐ No.

In Document O, is it possible to find the word AFGHANISTAN?
- ☐ Yes.
- ☐ No.

What other sites would likely make exciting scenes for the game
described in Document O?

_____

_____

_____

Of the characters from Documents N and O, which of them is the
most virtuous?
- ☐ Alabaster Wight
- ☐ Asana
- ☐ Auslander
- ☐ Garrote
- ☐ Jerboa
- ☐ Maya
- ☐ Pulmo
- ☐ Vergiften

Explain your answer to the previous question.

_____

_____

_____

Please do not write in this space.

Level VIII: Intelligence
Examination for Promotion
EXFP-LVVIII

Pike County Super Services Div.

You are taking the Level VIII Examination for Promotion because the Pike County Super Services Division has determined that there is a need for a Level VIII Superhero. You have successfully passed the interview and you are still a potential candidate for the position.

After a brief skills review, you'll need to successfully complete three live simulation test scenarios and the Level VIII Psychological Assessment in order to be promoted to Level VIII.

Skills Review
Review the skills you focused on in training before continuing.

Your Level VIII Superhero training focused on:

- Villain boss encounters.
- Strategy and tactics.
- Team problem solving.
- Extraterrestrial diplomacy.

Scenarios

You are required to pass all three VCR (Virtual Combat Room) scenarios before moving on to the Level VIII Psychological Assessment. For each scenario, a passing grade is 70 points.

Scenario 22: The Labyrinth
Objective: Get through the labyrinth.

Points		
	100	Labyrinth navigated within 1:00 minute
	90	Labyrinth navigated within 10:00 minutes
	80	Labyrinth navigated within 20:00 minutes
	70	Labyrinth navigated within 30:00 minutes
20 bonus points awarded for not using any super powers		
10 bonus points awarded for avoiding injury		

Scenario 23: Who Shot the President?
Objective: Analyze 174 photos taken on November 22, 1963, and then determine who shot the president.

Points		
	100	Correct analysis within 10:00 minutes
	90	Correct analysis within 30:00 minutes
	80	Correct analysis within 2 hours
	70	Correct analysis within 8 hours
10 bonus points awarded for determining what hospital the fourth person from the right in photo #153 was born in		
-10 points for each wrong guess		

Scenario 24: The Smart Villain
Objective: Defeat the villain in five out of six board games of the villain's choosing.

Points	100	Villain defeated in all six board games
	70	Villain defeated in five of six board games
-50 points for being caught cheating		

Level VIII Psychological Assessment

EXFP-LVVIII-C

The Level VIII Psychological Assessment is given on the following pages. There is no time limit for completion of this assessment, but the length of time you take will be recorded and considered along with your responses.

Directions

Read Documents P, Q, and R, and then answer the related questions. There are no right or wrong answers. A Reference Sheet has been included as an optional aid. Researching related people and events in the Hall of Humanity's archives is encouraged and can help you, but is not required.

Grading

The Super Services Division will evaluate your responses with guidance from a panel of peers at Level IX or higher. A passing grade will be acknowledged with a pay increase and official promotion to Level VIII duties.

Record the date and time before you begin.

Year	Month	Day	Hour	Minute	AM/PM

Reference Sheet
EXFP-LVVIII-D

Document P was discovered in an abandoned file cabinet in an alley behind X-Stream Copies, two days after Jake Bonson left his position as manager there. Bonson does not confirm nor deny that he wrote Document P, though the document credits him as the author.

Real Name	Superhero Name	Position
Jake	N/A	Civilian, manager
Irma	Protea	Level VIII Superhero
Tamara	Tamara	Level VII Superhero
Jerboa	Jerboa	Level III Superhero

Document P

Freak
By Jake Bonson

ork.

Today I am going to w

ill everything to myself.

As my sole inheritor I'll b

orrow the form of a body.

I'll give s

ickness respectability.

Machines will give qu

otes for those six feet under.

I'll write people n

agged by pop culture.

Meaning is b

inary as one is next to nothing.

Reproduction is to ord

er copying.

This job has confiscated the las

t of my control.

It's ou

t.

Document Q

a normal quiet

Irma says, I want out of
this world
now

Irma passes out

we
do
think, Tamara says   we
sometimes
laugh, Irma says

clouds

rain

one of the tables
is about to lose
it

a skinny, bearded man grabs
another man's table

Tamara and Jerboa split
him   Irma stands up, walks by
the man

his sandwich is
a turkey with everything

Document R

lunch

the business   I don't enjoy
anymore
Tamara says
don't be silly
napkins
are
a business,
you
are a business, Jerboa says, but
it works   that's a guaranteed
for sure

block the light
from coming into the café
Tamara says
she looks over at
that guy over there
his lunch, Tamara says
makes me angry

the sandwich off
and runs

after
the next table
is in shock

gone   Irma says, what'd you have?
Irma walks to the counter
to order

Level VIII

Psychological Assessment Questions

Form **2410-145**
RC3-990192

Name:	ID:
County: **Pike County**	Date:

How to fill out this form:
- For multiple choice questions, completely fill the box to the left of your choice.
- For write-in answers, please print legibly in the space provided.

Does Document P make sense?
- ☐ Yes.
- ☐ No.
- ☐ It depends on your perspective.

How is Document P meant to be read?
- ☐ Read all lines once, highest to lowest.
- ☐ Read each line on the left twice, once with each possible ending, highest to lowest.
- ☐ It's not meant to be read any one way.
- ☐ There is not enough information to figure it out.

Based on the information in Document P, which of the following statements about Jake Bonson are most likely true? (Select up to four.)
- ☐ Jake Bonson is intelligent.
- ☐ Jake Bonson would benefit from counseling.
- ☐ Jake Bonson has strong feelings about his career choices.
- ☐ Jake Bonson smokes marijuana.
- ☐ Jake Bonson owns cats.
- ☐ Everything is out of Jake Bonson's control.

Did you figure out Documents Q and R?
- ☐ Yes.
- ☐ No.
- ☐ I don't understand the question.

At the end of Document R, why does Irma go up to the counter to order?
- ☐ She wants a warm beverage.
- ☐ She is hungry and wants something to eat.
- ☐ She intends to replace the sandwich.
- ☐ She wants to be gone, like the sandwich.

Of the characters from Documents P, Q, and R, which of them is the most intelligent?
- ☐ Irma
- ☐ Jake Bonson
- ☐ Jerboa
- ☐ Tamara

Explain your answer to the previous question.

_____
_____
_____
_____

RC3-990192

Form 2410-145

Continued on other side

Please do not write in this space.

Level IX: Leadership

Examination for Promotion

EXFP-LVIX

You are taking the Level IX Examination for Promotion because the Pike County Super Services Division has determined that there is a need for a Level IX Superhero. You have successfully passed the interview and you are still a potential candidate for the position.

After a brief skills review, you'll need to successfully complete three live simulation test scenarios and the Level IX Psychological Assessment in order to be promoted to Level IX.

Skills Review
Review the skills you focused on in training before continuing.

Your Level IX Superhero training focused on:

- Issuing orders.
- Negotiations.
- Hiring.
- Optimizing the skills and abilities of a team.

Scenarios

You are required to pass all three VCR (Virtual Combat Room) scenarios before moving on to the Level IX Psychological Assessment. For each scenario, a passing grade is 70 points.

Scenario 25: The Quest
Objective: Lead a team of four amateur mountain climbers and one goat from base camp to the top of Mount Everest. It's allowed for one of the mountain climbers to die without summiting, but the goat must survive and make it to the top.

Points	100	Summit reached by the goat and all climbers, without injury
	85	Summit reached by the goat and all climbers, with some injuries
	70	Summit reached by the goat and all but one of the climbers
10 bonus points awarded for not hiring Sherpa guides		
20 bonus points awarded for not using any super powers		

Scenario 26: The Team Meeting

Objective: Lead the team meeting. Include an opportunity for everyone to share what they've been working on. Resolve all outstanding issues and delegate future tasks. Achieve a Satisfactory or higher rating from each team member on your management skills.

Points	100	Objectives met, meeting adjourned within 50:00 minutes
	90	Objectives met, meeting adjourned within 55:00 minutes
	80	Objectives met, meeting adjourned within 1 hour
	70	Objectives met
10 bonus points awarded for keeping the entire team awake		
-50 points for using violence		

Scenario 27: The Villain Team

Objective: Lead a team of Superheroes in defeating a team of villains.

Points	100	Villains defeated, no injuries on either side
	93	Villains defeated, no Superhero injuries
	86	Villains defeated, no critical Superhero injuries
	78	Villains defeated, critical Superhero injuries but no Superhero deaths
	70	Villains defeated, critical injuries and one or more Superhero deaths
10 bonus points awarded for maintaining the new condition of all costumes		

Level IX Psychological Assessment

EXFP-LVIX-C

The Level IX Psychological Assessment is given on the following pages. There is no time limit for completion of this assessment, but the length of time you take will be recorded and considered along with your responses.

Directions

Read Documents S, T, U, and V, and then answer the related questions. There are no right or wrong answers. A Reference Sheet has been included as an optional aid. Researching related people and events in the Hall of Humanity's archives is encouraged, can help you, and may or may not be required for passing.

Grading

The Super Services Division will evaluate your responses with guidance from a panel of peers at Level IX or higher. A passing grade will be acknowledged with a pay increase and official promotion to Level IX duties.

Record the date and time before you begin.

Year	Month	Day	Hour	Minute	AM/PM

Reference Sheet

EXFP-LVIX-D

Real Name	Superhero Name	Position
Robert	Alabaster Wight	Level VI Superhero
Pulmo	Pulmo	Level IX Superhero
Jerboa	Jerboa	Level IV Superhero
Garrote	Garrote	Level VIII Superhero
Irma	Protea	Level VIII Superhero*
Carver	Carver	Level V Superhero
Lage	N/A	Class A villain
Sallah	Sallah	Resident Superhero
Jake	N/A	Civilian, unemployed
Pierre Gourmont	N/A	Civilian, unemployed

*When Document U was written, Irma had resigned her position as a Level VIII Superhero, had served as a Vision Implementation Specialist, and had recently become unemployed.

Document S

Title: Support

Panel 1. On a city block that looks like it's been heavily smashed up, six Superheroes converge on one villain. Prominent on the block is a six-story building. It has a clothing store on the first floor with mannequins in the windows. The six Superheroes advance.

The largest of the heroes is ALABASTER WIGHT. He is a human made of alabaster stone, a dichotomy of strength and smooth, ornate beauty. He is large and strong.

PULMO is a humanoid extraterrestrial from another planet. He is on a small one-person flying machine and is closer to the villain than anyone else.

JERBOA is young. She's flying, which she does by creating and riding small wind currents.

GARROTE is a gritty motorcycle freak. He's not muscular, just kind of big. He's on his motorcycle, pulling up to the curb.

PROTEA has randomly rotating super powers and right now her powers are acrobatics and super strength. She is leaping onto the scene.

CARVER is a man with bits of fur sticking out of his costume. He is barefoot and running.

The villain is LAGE. He is firing concussive energy beams out of his hands. He wears an electro-suit.

CAPTION: THAT'S ME, THE GUY THAT LOOKS LIKE ALABASTER STONE.

CAPTION: THIS COULD BE A LONG DAY.

Panel 1. Lage fires an energy beam at Pulmo, hitting him square in the chest and knocking him off his flying machine.

Panel 2. Pulmo is propelled through the front window of the clothing store, smashing through a central support pillar.

Panel 3. Pulmo crumples against an interior wall.

CAPTION: GREAT. PULMO JUST TOOK OUT A SUPPORT BEAM --

Panel 4. Jerboa hovers above the action while Alabaster Wight starts walking toward the clothing store.

CAPTION: -- WHICH MEANS I KNOW WHAT I'LL BE DOING FOR THE REST OF THE FIGHT.

JERBOA: AL!

ALABASTER WIGHT: I'M ON IT.

Panel 1. Alabaster Wight steps through the hole in the glass window of the clothing store.

CAPTION: FANTASTIC. SIX MONTHS WITH US AND SHE'S ALREADY GIVING ORDERS.

Panel 2. Alabaster Wight stands in the spot where the support beam used to be, lifting his arms. There are cracks in the ceiling suggesting a possible cave-in. Pulmo picks himself up off the floor nearby.

CAPTION: NOW THE OTHERS WILL BE TOO BUSY EVACUATING THE BUILDING TO DO ANYTHING ABOUT LAGE.

Panel 3. Alabaster Wight is firmly in place, holding up the building by acting as a temporary support beam. He can still see outside through the large display windows. Pulmo is standing, dusting himself off.

CAPTION: AT LEAST I CAN STILL SEE THE ACTION.

PULMO: THAT WASN'T VERY POLITE.

Panel 1. Outside the clothing store, Pulmo hops on his flying machine. Jerboa floats toward a fifth story window where a man is waving at her in panic. Protea leaps toward the fourth floor where a woman is climbing out of a window. Garrote is on foot now. He and Carver advance toward Lage from opposite sides.

JERBOA: FLIERS, EVACUATE THAT BUILDING BEFORE IT COLLAPSES!

Panel 2. Garrote taunts Lage to get his attention while Carver gets closer to the villain from behind.

GARROTE: TRY THOSE FORCE BEAMS ON ME. I'M NOT TICKLISH.

Panel 1. Carver's mouth is open in anticipation. He is about to chop Lage's neck with his hand. Lage is still looking at Garrote (off panel). Energy is gathering around Lage's fists.

LAGE: YOU WANT SOME OF THIS?

Panel 2. Carver's hand is about a foot away from Lage. Electricity jumps out of Lage's suit to Carver's hand, electrocuting Carver's body. Carver's teeth are visible and a piece of his tongue falls to the ground. Alabaster Wight watches.

CAPTION: BAD NEWS. OUR VILLAIN HAS AN ELECTRO-SUIT.

Panel 3. Garrote runs toward Lage while Lage watches Carver crumple to the ground.

CAPTION: AS LUCK WOULD HAVE IT, ELECTRIC SHOCKS DON'T HURT ME, BUT I'M STUCK HOLDING UP THIS BUILDING.

Panel 4. Lage blasts Garrote with his force beam.

Panel 1. This frame is black except for two eyeholes (Alabaster Wight's perspective, looking out through the broken window of the clothing store). Maintain this convention for every panel on this page.

Garrote is flying through the air in the left eyehole. In the right eyehole, Lage is standing outside the clothing store, across the street.

CAPTION: OH, CRAP.

Panel 2. Same as the previous frame, except Garrote is nowhere to be seen and Lage is now looking directly at Alabaster Wight.

CAPTION: WHY DO I FEEL LIKE THE LAST HOG IN A SLAUGHTERHOUSE?

Panel 3. Same as the previous frame, except now Lage is closer, walking across the street, still looking directly at Alabaster Wight.

CAPTION: HE'S GOING TO BLAST ME AND THE BUILDING WILL COLLAPSE AND HUNDREDS OF PEOPLE WILL DIE.

Panel 4. Same as the previous frame, except now Lage is just outside the clothing store window and energy is gathering around his hands. He is smiling.

CAPTION: AND I PROBABLY WON'T FEEL A THING.

Panel 1. This panel is entirely black except for the narration.

CAPTION: I DON'T EVEN KNOW WHY I DO THIS.

CAPTION: PEOPLE ARE UNDESERVING MONSTERS. WHY BOTHER?

CAPTION: IT'S NOT BECAUSE THEY'RE CUTE.

CAPTION: THEY'RE NOT.

CAPTION: MAYBE I JUST HAVE A DEATH WISH.

CAPTION: OR MAYBE I DO IT BECAUSE I UNDERSTAND THAT PEOPLE, HOWEVER ILL-EQUIPPED, HAVE THE RESPONSIBILITY OF CARRYING THE SEED OF LIFE TO OTHER PLANETS, AND ON TO THE REST OF THE GALAXY AND THAT THIS IS EARTH'S WISH SO THAT SHE WILL NOT DIE WITH THE SUN.

CAPTION: SURE. THAT'S WHY I DO IT.

Panel 1. This frame is black except for two eyeholes (Alabaster Wight's perspective, looking out through the broken window of the clothing store). Maintain this convention for every panel on this page.

Lage clutches his head in his hands, still standing outside the clothing store.

LAGE: YAAAARRGGHH!

CAPTION: SAVED. LOOKS LIKE OUR RESIDENT TELEPATH FROM THE MIDDLE EAST --

Panel 2. Lage has fallen to the ground. Sallah appears right beside him, slightly transparent still.

SALLAH is thin and wears a cloak.

CAPTION: -- HAS ARRIVED FROM THE TWENTY-TWO CAR PILE-UP ACROSS TOWN.

Panel 3. Sallah extends his arm toward Lage, who is already moving again.

Panel 4. Electricity jumps from Lage's suit to Sallah's arm and jolts Sallah's entire body.

CAPTION: AH, CRAP.

Panel 1. Sallah falls to the ground. Lage is getting up.

CAPTION: THAT'S MY FAULT. I'M STANDING HERE DOING NOTHING --

Panel 2. Lage looks at Alabaster Wight again, energy gathering around his hands.

CAPTION: -- AND I DON'T EVEN THINK TO WARN SALLAH ABOUT THE ELECTRO-SUIT.

PROTEA (OP): HEY LAGE!

Panel 3. Lage looks toward Protea, who is in the process of throwing a lightning rod at Lage. The lightning rod is tied to a power line.

CAPTION: SMART. SHE'S TRYING TO FRY THE ELECTRO-SUIT.

Panel 4. Lage takes the lightning rod in the middle of his chest. Electricity surrounds his body. He is writhing in pain, but still standing.

LAGE: <u>AAARRRGGGH</u>!

Panel 5. Lage stands hunched over. The lightning rod is on the ground now, sparking.

CAPTION: NICE TRY, PROTEA. BUT NOW LAGE IS EVEN ANGRIER.

Panel 1. Lage stands up straight. He looks at Protea, energy gathering around his hands.

LAGE: <u>NOW YOU'RE DEAD</u>.

Panel 2. Protea is hurled across the street by a force beam from Lage.

Panel 3. Protea crumples into a car. Lage walks toward her. Alabaster Wight watches.

CAPTION: SHE'S TOAST. AND I CAN'T DO A THING.

Panel 1. Lage stands over Protea, energy gathering around his hands.

GARROTE (OP): HEY ELECTRO-BOY!

Panel 2. Lage is not distracted by Garrote's taunting. He aims his hands at Protea's face. Alabaster Wight watches.

CAPTION: LAGE WANTS PROTEA OUT OF THE WAY. PERMANENTLY.

Panel 3. Garrote's motorcycle suddenly smashes into Lage.

Panel 4. Lage is on the ground, near Garrote's motorcycle, already starting to get up. Garrote approaches.

GARROTE: I MEAN <u>YOU</u>, SHOCK MONKEY!

CAPTION: THINGS ARE PRETTY BAD WHEN GARROTE'S DESPERATE ENOUGH TO THROW HIS OWN MOTORCYCLE.

Panel 1. Lage is standing, arms outstretched as if he were on a cross, energy gathering around his hands. Garrote is ready for action as they face off, gunslinger-style, in the middle of the street.

Panel 2. Garrote dodges Lage's blast, leaping out of the way.

CAPTION: GARROTE'S TRYING TO DISTRACT HIM UNTIL THE BUILDING CAN BE EVACUATED.

Panel 3. Garrote dodges Lage's blast again, leaping the other direction.

CAPTION: BUT HE CAN'T DODGE FOREVER.

Panel 4. Garrote catches Lage's next beam in the chest and it forces him back, through the air.

GARROTE: OOF!

Panel 1. Garrote flies through the window of a pub, landing against the bar. A mop sticks out of a bucket nearby.

Panel 2. Lage approaches the pub. Garrote starts to get up. He's looking at the mop.

Panel 3. Garrote grabs the mop. Lage is close, now, with energy gathering around his hands.

CAPTION: THINGS ARE EVEN WORSE WHEN GARROTE CONTEMPLATES USING A MOP AS A WEAPON.

Panel 4 (inset panel 5). Garrote snaps the handle of the mop on his knee, breaking it in two.

Panel 5. Garrote puts the handle end of the mop in his mouth, biting it.

Panel 1. Lage fires a beam of energy at Garrote who dodges it by throwing himself on the bar, landing on his back.

Panel 2. Garrote reaches for a bottle of whiskey.

Panel 3 (inset panel 2). Garrote breaks the fat end of the bottle on the edge of the bar.

Panel 4. Before Lage can get enough charge for another force beam, Garrote shoves the broken whiskey bottle into Lage's stomach. While Garrote and Lage are being electrocuted, blood spills from Lage's wound.

Panel 1. Garrote and Lage are on the floor of the bar, unconscious.

CAPTION: SMART. GARROTE PUNCTURED THE ELECTRO-SUIT SO LAGE WAS NO LONGER PROTECTED FROM THE SHOCKS.

Panel 2. Alabaster Wight is still standing in the middle of the clothing store, holding up the ceiling. A mannequin is on either side of him. His face is expressionless. Broken glass litters the sidewalk and interior of the store.

Panel 3. Same as the previous frame, except now someone is pushing a broom across the sidewalk.

Panel 4. Same as the previous frame, except now Jerboa is flying in through the broken storefront window.

JERBOA: THERE ARE STILL A FEW PEOPLE IN THE BUILDING. NEED ME TO FIND SOMEONE TO RELIEVE YOU?

Panel 1. Jerboa and Alabaster Wight talk, face to face.

ALABASTER WIGHT: THAT'S ALL RIGHT. I CAN WAIT FOR THE FIRE DEPARTMENT TO PROP THIS UP.

JERBOA: I COULD HAVE GUESSED --

Panel 2. Same as the previous frame, except Jerboa's face shows a sneering smile.

JERBOA: -- REMAINING UNMOVED IS ONE OF YOUR SPECIAL GIFTS.

ALABASTER WIGHT: DON'T MAKE ME LAUGH. I MIGHT DROP A BUILDING ON OUR HEADS.

Panel 3. Jerboa is on her way out, looking back at Alabaster Wight.

JERBOA: THAT MIGHT BE JUST WHAT YOU NEED.

Document T

bonson2@hotmail.com

Jake Bonson
Program Administrator

Disciplines/Specialties
- Statistics
- Probability
- Philosophy
- Primates

Education
- MA, Philosophy
  University of
  New Mexico, 2006
- MS, Probability
  and Statistics
  University of Illinois
  at Chicago, 2002
- BS, Statistics
  University of
  Minnesota, 2000

Safety Certifications
- CPR & First Aid, 2010

Summary of Experience

Jake Bonson is a high level program administrator who recently spearheaded the Great Monkey Project to resounding success, thousands of years ahead of schedule. Using an esteemed wealth of knowledge about statistics and probability that informs a personal philosophy of success and determination, Bonson gets the job done on all fronts.

Administrative Experience
The Great Monkey Project, Pittsburgh, PA, 2009 to 2010

Bonson initiated and oversaw the Great Monkey Project. His administrative duties brought 40,000 monkeys to Pittsburgh from all over the world, gathered over 220 text-match recognition specialists from across the country, and produced a final product literally thousands of years ahead of schedule, according to all known calculated probability of success assessments.

Managing the Great Monkey Project was no less challenging than managing a small town. And in many ways, the Great Monkey Project was a small town—a town that produced 36,000 pounds of waste per day (most of it feces), consumed 22% of Pittsburgh's electricity, and processed 170 reams of paper per hour. Bonson created the magic formula

Published Works

- "Expecting a 0.0000001 Probability Event" -*Probability Quarterly*, 2008
- "Randomness in Motor Skills of Primates" -*The Journal of Obscure Neuroscience*, 2004
- "Monkey Excretions, August" -*Probability Quarterly*, 2002
- "Monkey Excretions, July" -*Probability Quarterly*, 2002

for success using a management ratio calculation based on his statistical research, which showed optimal results at a specific ratio of human managers per computational devices per monkeys. He was instrumental in hiring all personnel, worked closely with computer scientists to program the computational instruments of analysis, and personally inspected every monkey involved in the project. Bonson also oversaw the smooth dismantling of the project after success was achieved.

Though the Great Monkey Project was only fully operational for less than two weeks, Bonson spearheaded efforts to support the project for over a year before it got underway. The Great Monkey Project required special city ordinances just to operate legally, which Bonson helped lobby and campaign for. The Great Monkey Project also required over $74 million of funding, which Bonson raised using completely original fundraising algorithms that dictated weekly goals and networking efforts. He also negotiated solutions to projected supply chain shortages (food, water, paper towels, and garbage bags) well before any such shortage could take place.

In summary, Jake Bonson can produce miracles thousands of years ahead of schedule, just as the Great Monkey Project did when monkey number 7,140 typed out a word-for-word duplicate of Hamlet during the second week of operation. Jake Bonson's promise to you is: "No statistical chance of failure will hold your project back from success as long as I'm in charge!"

Other Work History

Manager at X-Stream Copies, Pittsburgh, PA, 2006 to 2008

- Developed outstanding team of copying professionals and print consultation experts.
- Created employee efficiency ratings and implemented rating system throughout entire region.
- Earned a 97.9% approval rating from coworkers, 96.4% approval from customers.

Nature Guide at Standing Tall Hikes, Australia, 2002 to 2003
- Led beginning level hikers on exciting and educational nature trips not longer than twenty minutes.
- Handled clients' paperwork for mutual satisfaction.
- Implemented office improvement plan.

Line Cook at Burger King, St. Paul, MN, 1997 to 1999
- Fed meat products into machines for maximum flame-broiled flavor.
- Constructed sandwiches with aplomb to the satisfaction of several hundred customers per shift.
- Maintained supply of condiments by slicing tomatoes, chopping onions, and opening 5-gallon pickle buckets without incident.

Document U

姓 名	Irma Sabo	性別	女
生日	1975年1月10日		
永久住址	███████████████		
電話	████████████		
E-mail	irmasabo@gmail.com		
最高學歷	德州白楊高度高中 (Alamo Heights High School)		
語言	英文、中文、手語		
專長	拳打腳踢、演講、體操、射箭、計畫管理、各種不同的臨時超能力		
興趣	無		
應徵職務	任何和猴子或和超極英雄無關的工作		
希望待遇	說真的 ，只要能讓我離開現在這個地方，我不在乎錢		

自傳

我有一個困苦的童年，在我十二歲之後，我被一個叫 Pulmo 的外星人撫養長大。 我住在一個孤立的海島上的一棟大豪宅。 我們成立了一個非法的超級英雄小組而且還因為使用我們的超能力被抓到很多次。到最後，在可能會死掉的威脅下，我們透過一個叫 Reuben 的代理人加入了一個正式超級英雄的組織。 幫助人是我的工作責任，所以我可以拿薪水，是還蠻不錯的。我被升到全職的超級英雄而且還晉級到第VIII級。然而，在一個特別辛苦的一天，實際上，對超級英雄來說，是個相當普通的星期六下午，我決定脫離這個組織，去找和這方面無關的工作。在我少數幾個和超級英雄無關的聯絡人之一有一個叫 Jake Bonson 的，他是大猴子計畫的負責人。 Bonson 給了我 Vision Implementation Specialist 的職位，也是這計畫的第二負責人。當然，如果妳／你有在看有關美國的新聞的話，妳／你就一定知道大猴子計畫在開始全能運作的二個星期內便停止了。所以現在的我，想盡辦法要離開匹茲堡，且能離的越遠越好。 請雇用我吧。

特別訓練
縫紉

學歷
我並沒有什麼高的學歷 ，但是我每隔幾個星期或幾個月就會擁有一個新的不同的超能力。 在我在白楊高度高中的時候，我得到了一個可以快速學會任何東西的超能力，所以我學了中文和一些高級算術。 然後，在我休學後，我在GED考試中拿了滿分。

工作經歷
大猴子計畫, Vision Implementation Specialist, 2009-2010
- 實施負責人的理念和夢想
- 與三十二個不同的公司協調總價值超過七千四百萬美元的貨運
- 我在這個計畫的籌備階段有快一年的時間， 但這計畫在開始全能運作的兩個星期內就停止了， 所以我離開了這個職位。

Pike County Super Services Division, Level VIII 超級英雄 2002-2009
- 救人
- 保護公共建築
- 捉拿壞人
- 幫助其他超級英雄
- 和其他超級英雄一起打擊罪犯和不公平
- 我離開這個工作因為我厭倦了一直救人，而且我不知道自己是不是真的救了她/他們，我也曾想過她/他們真的值得救嗎？在當我對這工作有許多疑惑時，Jake 給我一個很好的工作機會。

Document V

Pierre Gourmont

pierre.gourmont@gmail.com

Summary
I am a positive-thinking, hard worker—dedicated to expanding my skills in a non-monkey environment!

Professional Experience

Special Clean-Up Technician
Emergency Monkey Clean-Up Team   March to a few days ago
- Aided in clean-up and disposal of over 36,000 monkey carcasses.
- Recorded and processed requests for reparations from citizens of Pittsburgh.
- Reason for leaving: Monkey clean-up team disbanded by mayor once situation was deemed under control.

Monkey Content Match Expert
Great Monkey Project   March
- Matched grammatically correct monkey-produced content to well-known literary works of importance using computer database and word processing skills.
- Discovered a 23-page excerpt of a relatively obscure Joan Lindsay text.
- Scanned pages of monkey-produced typewriting into a computer database.
- Assisted in feeding monkeys (numbers 22,361 through 22,400).
- Reason for leaving: Project head ceased operation of project by turning off all grid power and opening great monkey doors.

Education
B.A. in English, Syracuse University, December 2009

References available upon request.

Level IX

Psychological Assessment Questions

Form **2410-146**
RC3-990194

Name:	ID:
County: **Pike County**	Date:

How to fill out this form:
- For multiple choice questions, completely fill the box to the left of your choice.
- For write-in answers, please print legibly in the space provided.

Which of the following characters from Document S is the most creative?
- ☐ Carver
- ☐ Garrote
- ☐ Jerboa
- ☐ Lage
- ☐ Protea

Which of the following characters from Document S do you think has the best sense of humor?
- ☐ Alabaster Wight
- ☐ Garrote
- ☐ Jerboa
- ☐ Pulmo
- ☐ Sallah

Judging only from the information in Documents T, U, and V, do you think the Great Monkey Project was a success?
- ☐ Yes.
- ☐ No.

Explain your answer to the previous question.

_____

_____

_____

_____

_____

_____

Using only the information in Documents T, U, and V, which person would you prefer to hire as a Superhero in your division?
- ☐ Irma Sabo
- ☐ Jake Bonson
- ☐ Pierre Gourmont

Of the characters from Documents S, T, U, and V, which of them would you choose to implement your vision?
- ☐ Alabaster Wight
- ☐ Carver
- ☐ Garrote
- ☐ Irma Sabo / Protea
- ☐ Jake Bonson
- ☐ Jerboa
- ☐ Lage
- ☐ Pierre Gourmont
- ☐ Pulmo
- ☐ Sallah

Of the characters from Documents S, T, U, and V, which of them is the best leader?
- ☐ Alabaster Wight
- ☐ Carver
- ☐ Garrote
- ☐ Irma Sabo / Protea
- ☐ Jake Bonson
- ☐ Jerboa
- ☐ Lage
- ☐ Pierre Gourmont
- ☐ Pulmo
- ☐ Sallah

Form 2410-146

Continued on other side

Explain your answer to the previous question.

_____

_____

_____

_____

_____

Please do not write in this space.

Form 2410-146

Level X: Invulnerability
Examination for Promotion
EXFP-LVX

Pike County Super Services Div.

You are taking the Level X Examination for Promotion because the Pike County Super Services Division has determined that there is a need for a Level X Superhero. You have successfully passed the interview and you are still a potential candidate for the position.

After a brief skills review, you'll need to successfully complete three live simulation test scenarios and the Level X Psychological Assessment in order to be promoted to Level X.

Skills Review
Review the skills you focused on in training before continuing.

Your Level X Superhero training focused on:

- CLASSIFIED
- CLASSIFIED
- CLASSIFIED
- CLASSIFIED

Scenarios

You are required to pass all three VCR (Virtual Combat Room) scenarios before moving on to the Level X Psychological Assessment. For each scenario, a passing grade is 70 points.

Scenario 28: The Nuclear Bomb
Objective: Survive the point blank range nuclear bomb explosion.

Points		
	100	Survival, no injury
	90	Survival, no critical injury
	80	Survival, with critical injuries
	70	Survival
10 bonus points awarded for mutating in a positive way		

Scenario 29: The Gauntlet
Objective: Rescue the baby from the hoard of vampires and deliver the baby unharmed to the parents. Rescue the parents and their baby from the extraterrestrial armada. Permanently stop the extraterrestrial armada from enslaving the planet. Retrieve six ounces of solid matter from the sun. Divert a Saturn-sized meteor from hitting the Earth.

Points		
	100	Objectives met within 10 hours
	90	Objectives met within 24 hours
	80	Objectives met within 2 days
	70	Objectives met within 3 days
30 bonus points awarded for not using any super powers		

Scenario 30: The Undefeatable Villain
Objective: Defeat the villain.

Points	100	CLASSIFIED
	90	CLASSIFIED
	80	CLASSIFIED
	70	CLASSIFIED
30 bonus points awarded for CLASSIFIED		

Level X Psychological Assessment

EXFP-LVX-C

The Level X Psychological Assessment is given on the following pages. There is no time limit for completion of this assessment, but the length of time you take will be recorded and considered along with your responses.

Directions

Read Documents W and X, and then answer the related questions. There are no right or wrong answers. A Reference Sheet has been included as an optional aid. Researching related people and events in the Hall of Humanity's archives is mandatory for passing.

Grading

The Super Services Division will evaluate your responses with guidance from a panel of peers at Level X or higher. A passing grade will be acknowledged with a pay increase and official promotion to Level X duties.

Record the date and time before you begin.

Year	Month	Day	Hour	Minute	AM/PM

Reference Sheet

Real Name	Superhero Name	Position
Sera	Asana	Level IX Superhero
Praxis	Praxis	Level X Superhero
Robert	Alabaster Wight	Level VI Superhero
Jake	N/A	Civilian, owner of business
Garrote	Garrote	Level VIII Superhero
Mike	N/A	Class B villain
Lage	N/A	Class A villain
Jerboa	Jerboa	Level IV Superhero
Irma	Protea	Level VIII Superhero
Pulmo	Pulmo	Level IX Superhero
Tamara	Tamara	Level VII Superhero
Pierre Gourmont	N/A	Civilian, independently wealthy
Maya	N/A	Civilian, paralegal
Nelson	Nelson	Civilian, explorer
Edward	Edward	Deceased
Carver	Carver	Level V Superhero
Sallah	Sallah	Resident Superhero
Jonesy	N/A	Civilian, program manager

Document W

The Transfer

Level IX Superhero Asana[1] was notified of the transfer's approval[2] by Super Courier[3], 0.78 seconds after the official decision was made at the Federal Bureau of Super Services[4] headquarters[5].

The transfer request was applied for by Asana, and fully supported by Praxis[6].

The going away party[7] was interrupted by an emergency[8].

No one was surprised.

1 Most of Asana's coworkers had called her Sera, until Alabaster Wight[9] asked her which she preferred at work (Asana), and then started a campaign[10] to get people to use Asana at work.
2 Superheroes are allowed and encouraged to transfer between county, state, and federal Superhero institutions[11] as part of the Independent Superhero Action Committee's River Waters Mandate[12].
3 Super Courier, Incorporated[13], is owned and operated by Jake Bonson and employs fewer than three people[14].
4 The Federal Bureau of Super Services was created as part of a three-part legislation regulating the appearance, behavior, and Superhero practices of all Superheroes. Its primary purpose is to recruit new Superheroes, track illegal uses of super powers[15], and prosecute criminals with super powers.
5 The Federal Bureau of Super Services headquarters is in a classified location[16].
6 Praxis always liked Asana because she rarely called for help[17].
7 Going away parties are not standard for county Superheroes transferring to state or federal level institutions[18], but Garrote[19] insisted.

8 The emergency began as a high-priority investigation of the Mike Barovich-Lage breakout, and developed into Pike County Super Services Division Level X Incident 1,292[20].

9 Alabaster Wight was once told by Jerboa that he would need to outgrow his sulky, negative attitude if he ever expected to get past Level VII[21].

10 Just before the time of her transfer, only 32% of Asana's coworkers called her Sera at work.

11 Transfer from a county level to a state or federal level almost always[22] results in a level or multi-level demotion[23].

12 The River Waters Mandate was a 572-point plan to facilitate communication between Superhero agencies. The River Waters Mandate implemented changes within the Superhero Level Authority that eventually succeeded[24] in standardizing Superhero ratings, improving Superhero methods of operation, and improving the Overall Effectiveness Rating (OER[25]) of every Superhero institution by at least 5% and in some cases by as much as 22%.

13 Super Courier, Incorporated made news headlines on its opening day of business by unveiling a service that could relay moderately-sized physical artifacts from point-to-point across the globe in less than one second[26].

14 Level VIII Superhero Protea was not one of the few employees of Super Courier, Incorporated, though she was offered a position there. She declined for personal reasons[27] though her recent reinstatement as a Level VIII Superhero perhaps also contributed to the decision.

15 Technically, all uses of super powers were made illegal unless officially employed as a Superhero, but the Federal Bureau of Super Services focuses prosecution on those doing forms of vigilante work[28].

16 Applicants invited to interview for positions offered through the Superhuman Resources Department of the Federal Bureau of Super Services must find the location of the headquarters or be disqualified[29].

17 No documented incidence of Asana calling for help exists in the Pike County Super Services Division's archives.

18 This is because a transfer up means the Superhero is more likely to die in Superhero service.

19 Garrote at first protested the transfer[30] but after hearing directly from Asana that it was what she wanted, he supported it completely.

20 The debriefing-in-progress for Level X Incident 1,292 is filed under level_x_001292.rtf.

21 To which, Alabaster Wight replied, "You may be right."[31]

22 Asana did not receive a level demotion.

23 The level ratings of all of the Superhero institutions are regulated by the Superhero Level Authority[32].

24 Critics of the River Waters Mandate claim that it discourages the proud tradition of true innovation that Superheroes have engaged in since their origin.

25 The OER is a statistic created by Jake Bonson that evaluates Superhero actions on a cost-benefit basis.

26 The expedient transportation of said physical artifacts was made possible by the creation of a machine[33] that Jake Bonson called the Hotel[34].

27 Rumors pinpointed Protea's personal reasons as being related to Pulmo's imminent departure from Earth[35], and Protea's desire to continue to surround

herself with the support structure that being a Superhero provided, rather than attempt to live as a civilian without other Superheroes' support[36].

28 This focus was a drastic revision of the original inclusive aim of the Federal Bureau of Super Services, cut back from its original ambitious goal of 100% enforcement, largely because of public reaction to U.S. vs. Alvin Rodgers-Dyson[37].

29 A saying among Superheroes suggests that once you find the Federal Bureau of Super Services headquarters, the hard part of the interview is over, but the saying isn't true.

30 Garrote's reason for protesting the transfer was that he knew Asana was being assigned to Federal Super Services Station 4A[38].

31 To which, Jerboa replied by complimenting him on his powers of perception in such a way that only years later would Alabaster Wight realize that the compliment was actually a scathing but accurate insult.

32 The Superhero Level Authority was created along with the Federal Bureau of Super Services as part of a three-part legislation regulating the appearance, behavior, and Superhero practices of all Superheroes. The Superhero Level Authority's primary purpose is to maintain Superhero evaluation and rating consistency between county, state, and federal levels.

33 The plans[39] for this machine were typed without error by monkey number 22,391 during the Great Monkey Project.

34 Jake Bonson called it the Hotel because the word "Hotel" was the title of the plans typed by monkey number 22,391. The title of the document was the only thing the monkey typed that didn't make sense.

35 Pulmo announced his imminent departure from Earth[40] as soon as he felt Protea was ready to make it on her own.

36 It helped that Protea's friend, Tamara, was still at the same division, though that changed soon after Protea's reinstatement[41].

37 U.S. vs. Alvin Rodgers-Dyson was an attempt by the Federal Bureau of Super Services to prosecute an autistic child for superhuman math calculations[42].

38 Federal Super Services Station 4A is a federal Superhero district well known as the only district without a Level X Superhero[43].

39 The plans themselves were discovered by Pierre Gourmont while scouring the Great Monkey Project's final print output for fun, during a fourteen week period between jobs. Bonson paid Gourmont an undisclosed amount as a finder's fee.

40 Pulmo was only on Earth in the first place because of bizarre readings[44] he picked up while circling the solar system, which had compelled him to investigate.

41 Tamara's ability to see into the future was partially at fault[45].

42 Former Level IV Administrative Assistant Maya was a paralegal at the firm that defended Alvin Rodgers-Dyson. In a letter of reference written by Level IX Attorney Ann Drake, Maya's work was praised as being "highly instrumental in rescuing Alvin Rodgers-Dyson and others in the same situation from certain and unjust peril."

43 While Garrote knew Federal Super Services Station 4A had no Level X Superhero on staff, he was unaware that Asana would be the district's only Level IX Superhero, and that she would effectively serve as the Level X-on-duty when Level X incidents were identified[46].

44 The readings were found to be emanating from Protea, who was a child at that time, during an especially long bout with an as-yet-uncontrollable telekinetic power[47].

45 Tamara had a future vision stability rating of 6.3 and a range of between 5 minutes and 50 years into the future until a blast suffered during Level X Incident 1,292 left her with a major concussion, at which time her future vision started to shift dramatically until she could see all the way to the end of time[48].

46 At Federal Super Services Station 4A, the rate of Level X situations is 1 per 1.83 days, the highest incidence ratio of all the districts.

47 Pulmo was able to use his extraterrestrial technology to dampen Protea's ability somewhat until she was able to control it[49].

48 After seeing the end of time[50], Tamara adopted a very lax stance on things mattering, and promptly retired from active duty[51].

49 Protea was able to control her powers within approximately two weeks, though three days after she mastered telekinesis, she lost that power and gained a new one[52].

50 Technically, what Tamara saw was not the end of time, but instead what she perceived as the end of time. Certain very small entities[53] still exist after the point of time in the future that Tamara labeled "the end of time."

51 Tamara continued to meet Protea for lunch from time to time.

52 Protea regularly but without consistent timing loses and gains powers as well as superhuman abilities.

53 One very small entity that still exists after the end of time is Nelson[54], who continues to shrink.

54 Asana never forgot about Nelson, or Edward, or anyone else[55].

55 Garrote noted Asana's thoughtfulness in his goodbye speech to Asana at the going away party. Then, he said, "Good luck, kiddo. It's going to be tough." [56] And Garrote knew what he was talking about, though Asana didn't, exactly.

56 To which Asana replied, "I know." And Asana knew what she was talking about, though Garrote didn't, exactly.

Document X

Summary—type up for the Commissioner:

Barovich had a stash.

Two confirmations that Barovich's dad created the pills in his lab, never sold them but some did leak out.

Pills give people temporary abilities: flight, heat stuff up with their hands, ability to throw fire balls.

Barovich's cell mate Hills saw Barovich smuggle pills in after Barovich was transferred to State.

Pills gave Barovich powers.

Barovich melted cell door.

Set fires as distractions throughout prison.

Apparently took 18 months to arrange.

Headed straight to Lage's cell in D block.

Still investigating Barovich's connection to Lage. Tenuous at best.

Enlisted help from Lage

Lage also made use of pills to benefit from powers.

Lage's cell mate Decker heard talk of destroying downtown as a sort of deal between the two.

The two escaped together.

Security camera footage shows Barovich and Lage took less than 5 minutes to melt their way out.

Seems to be key in Lage agreeing to help Barovich out with some sort of plan.

Files from Hall of Humanity's archives indicate Lage has uncontrollable urge to destroy civilization.

Very likely pills were offered in exchange for Lage's services in destroying downtown.

If Barovich and Lage made a deal, Lage was getting everything he wanted.

Strong motive: Barovich's dad killed by Carver.

Outlandish theory: Barovich and Lage may have caused large scale incident for the sole purpose of drawing Carver to the scene to murder him and avenge Barovich's father. IMPLAUSIBLE!!!

I spotted Lage from two districts over. There he was, hurling fire ball after fire ball at the sprawling collection of mighty skyscrapers.

Lage is downtown, I thought to my fellow on-duty Superheroes. *He's flying over District 12 and throwing fire balls. I do hope everyone has a fresh flame-retardant coating on their uniforms.*

I sensed their minds spring into action. Not even twenty seconds later, Jerboa alighted on the top of the building where I was perched.

"Let's go get him," she said.

She snatched me up and flew us in seconds to where Lage was loitering. He was just about to put another fire ball through a window of the Staunch Life building, when he spied us!

SHWAAAA!!!

A super-heated fire ball flew past. Jerboa dodged it easily, despite carrying me while she flew.

Meanwhile, I used my powerful mental abilities to give our assailant the biggest headache he's ever had—bigger than the one I gave him during our first encounter, so many months ago. It worked...for a while. His altitude began to drop as he lost concentration, then he refocused and from his hands sprang forth an enormous wall of fire!

I was too engaged with his mental aura to be able to teleport us to safety!

"Sallah," Jerboa said. "I can't dodge that!"

Never fear, for in the nick of time, Pulmo appeared on his lightning-quick flying machine. He intercepted the wall of fire and absorbed it with some sort of installed gadget—an alien device created using the learnings of an interplanetary culture.

But the fire was too much for the machine! An energy overload viciously shorted out the machine, and Pulmo began to fall!

Since I'd been given a brief respite from my mental attack, I was now ready and able to teleport once more.

I've got him, I thought to Jerboa. I didn't have time for my usual eloquence.

In a flash, I teleported to Pulmo's plummeting body, wrapped my hand around his arm, and then teleported us both to a safe landing area: an emergency landing mat I have set up for just these types of emergencies.

After I regained my sense of gravity, I found Pulmo unable to respond to my thought-queries. Upon closer inspection, I realized that the machine in which he places so much faith had backfired from the excess energy and given him quite a shock.

I instantly teleported him to the emergency room of the county hospital. The staff quickly assisted me in getting Pulmo comfortably rested on a stretcher, while my perceptive mind abilities detected a rude comment from one of the nurses. *Oh, great. Another Superhero*, thought the nurse, the sarcasm dripping wet insults all over the tiled floor.

Here I must digress from the story in order to elaborate on the downfall of mind reading as a super power. One might think it's a very handy skill to have, whereas knowing what people are thinking can be a valuable asset to any objective-oriented individual. However, it is not the case that mind reading can be in any way a clear indication of anyone's character, or of a person's predisposition toward making any specific action. In fact, in many situations, the thoughts of human beings are merely an unwelcome and

Post-Battle Analysis—Time Grid, Sheet 7

	12:32:03-05	12:32:06-08	12:32:09-11	12:32:12-14	12:32:15-17
Lage	Shoots fire ball	Shoots fire ball	Shoots fire ball	Shoots fire ball	Shoots fire ball
Incidentals	N/A	Staunch Life hit by fire ball	Construction site hit by fire ball	Statue in plaza hit by fire ball	Cassandra Tower hit by fire ball
Mike Barovich	Hiding	Hiding	Hiding	Hiding	Hiding
Sallah	At hospital	At hospital	At hospital	At hospital	At hospital
Jerboa	Hit by fire ball	Crash lands on rooftop	Unconscious	Unconscious	Unconscious
Pulmo	Unconscious, at hospital	Unconscious, at hospital	Unconscious, at hospital	Unconscious, at hospital	Unconscious, at hospital
Asana	En route by foot, on rooftop	Steps off rooftop	Falling, prepares to execute action TKV356-D7	Lands on titanium-reinforced spring loaded awning to complete action TKV356-D7	Executes aerial somersaults, lands on back of Garrote's moving motorcycle

Garrote	En route by motorcycle	En route by motorcycle	En route by motorcycle	En route by motorcycle	En route by motorcycle
Alabaster Wight	En route by foot	En route by foot	En route by foot	En route by foot	En route by foot
Protea	En route by taxi	En route by taxi	En route by taxi	En route by taxi	En route by taxi
Tamara	En route by taxi	En route by taxi	En route by taxi	En route by taxi	En route by taxi
Praxis	En route by public transit	En route by public transit	En route by public transit	En route by public transit	En route by public transit
Carver	Off duty	Off duty	Off duty	Off duty	Off duty

Created by Lage

Post-Battle Analysis—Time Grid, Sheet 8

	12:32:18-20	12:32:21-23	12:32:24-26	12:32:27-29	12:32:30-32
Lage	Shoots fire ball	Hit by leg clamp, clamp tied to cable	Attempts to get clamp off	Flies sporadically to shake Asana off cable	Limited motion, cable tied to steel girder of construction site
Incidentals	Nell Center hit by fire ball	ATM at corner of Dallas and 4th hit by fire ball	N/A	N/A	N/A
Mike Barovich	Hiding	Hiding	Hiding	Hiding	Hiding
Sallah	At hospital	At hospital	At hospital	At hospital	At hospital
Jerboa	Unconscious	Unconscious	Unconscious	Unconscious	Unconscious
Pulmo	Unconscious, at hospital	Unconscious, at hospital	Unconscious, at hospital	Unconscious, at hospital	Unconscious, at hospital

	En route by motorcycle, shoots cable from Super Shot 9000c	Holds on to other end of cable, lifted off of motorcycle	In air, holding on to other end of cable	In air, prepares to execute action HLQ209-F2	Executes action HLQ209-F2 using steel girder of construction site
Asana					
Garrote	En route by motorcycle	En route by motorcycle	En route by motorcycle	En route by motorcycle	En route by motorcycle
Alabaster Wight	En route by foot	En route by foot	En route by foot	En route by foot	En route by foot
Protea	En route by taxi	En route by taxi	En route by taxi	En route by taxi	En route by taxi
Tamara	En route by taxi	En route by taxi	En route by taxi	En route by taxi	En route by taxi
Praxis	En route by public transit	En route by public transit	En route by public transit	En route by public transit	En route by public transit
Carver	Off duty	Off duty	Off duty	Off duty	Off duty

Created by Lage

ACTION HLQ209-F2

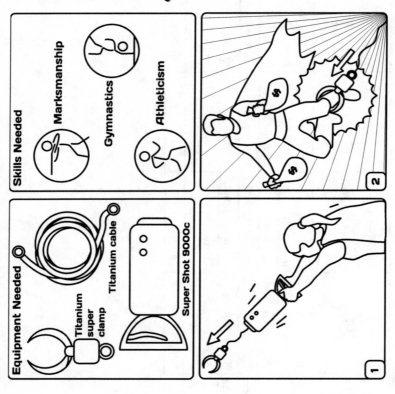

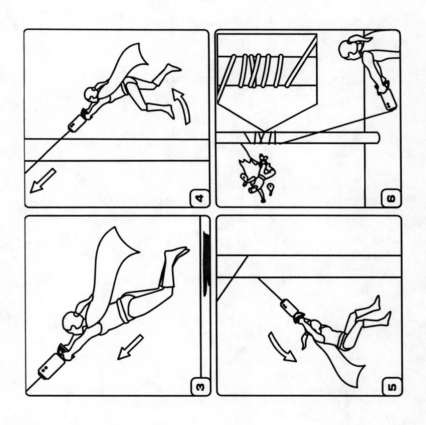

Level X Incident 1,292: The Musical

                          LAGE
Asana may have tied me to this girder
But my fire can surely still hurt her.
                    (Shoots fire ball)

                         ASANA
Garrote, a fire ball's on its way!

                        GARROTE
Get behind my bike and we'll be okay.

                         (ASANA and GARROTE take
                         cover behind the motorcycle.
                         The fire ball dissipates when
                         it hits the motorcycle.)

                          LAGE
What is this madness? Your bike should be toast!
How do you own a motorcycle fire cannot roast?

                         ASANA
About your motorcycle, Garrote—I can't help but like
That fire resistant enamel—

                        GARROTE
Hey, I love my bike!

                         (Enter ALABASTER WIGHT, from
                         stage right)

                    ALABASTER WIGHT
You might not remember me, Lage,
Because during our first encounter, I couldn't engage.
Your wicked actions took out a support beam
And I was the only one on my team
That could hold a building up with my muscle
While the rest of you had a long tussle.
So it's good we meet again, here in downtown
And this time, I promise you, I'll take you down.

Level X Incident 1,292: The Musical

                          LAGE
Fire balls would probably bounce right off your skin,
But watch while I create a hole for you to fall in.

                              (LAGE blasts a hole in the
                              street right under ALABASTER
                              WIGHT, who falls in.)

                     ALABASTER WIGHT
Curse my rotten luck—I'm trapped again,
Unable to help attack or defend
My teammates, who deserve the absolute best—
I'll never pass that Level Seven test!

                          MIKE
                     (Still in hiding)
So far events match the plan in my head.
But where is Carver? I want him dead!

                              (Enter PROTEA and TAMARA in
                              a taxi, from stage right.
                              They hop out of the taxi.)

                         PROTEA
I have a new power—got it just today.
Lage, feel the wrath of my vicious poison spray!

                              (PROTEA shoots water out
                              of her hands at LAGE. LAGE
                              counters by shooting a stream
                              of fire that evaporates the
                              water.)

                         TAMARA
I thought it was only water coming out of your hands.

                         PROTEA
Hush—if he finds out, it'll ruin the plan.

Level X Incident 1,292: The Musical

                    LAGE
I don't know what she's shooting forth like a spout.
But I sure as ~~XXXX~~ don't want to find out.
            HECK

                    (GARROTE and ASANA sneak up
                    on LAGE from behind.)

                    GARROTE
                    (Grabs LAGE)
I've got him, Asana. Now put him to rest!

                    ASANA
No problem, Garrote. I always do my best.

                    (ASANA knocks LAGE out with
                    a punch. Garrote and Asana
                    high five each other.)

                    MIKE
                    (Still in hiding)
Noooooooooooooooooooooooooooo!
Lage, you fool! Don't pass out like that!
My plan isn't finished—where is Carver at?

                    (Enter SALLAH, from stage
                    right. JERBOA regains
                    consciousness and stands
                    up.)

                    MIKE (CONTINUED)
Sallah has returned. Jerboa's awake.
How long is Carver going to take?
So many Superheroes, all in one place.
Yet where is the one that I want to deface?
There's only one thing to do, to draw Carver near—
I'll blast all these heroes—everyone here.
If I blow up these heroes, he's sure to show up.
And I can do it, if I take every pill in this cup.
I'll overdose, that's true, but that's a small detail.
I will kill the one who killed my father, without fail.

Level X Incident 1,292: The Musical

                    MIKE (CONTINUED)
Once Carver is dead, I don't care what will be.
So long as he's dead, I don't care if this kills me.

                         (MIKE swallows all of the
                         pills, and then comes out of
                         his hiding spot to reveal
                         himself. He raises his arms,
                         and then a blinding flash
                         of light knocks all the
                         Superheroes to the ground.)

                    END OF ACT II

Ethan—you're Lage and you're unconscious so at this point in the play you can't stand up and shout "Bad guys win! Bad guys win!" Please do me a favor and practice not doing that when you rehearse this at home.

Interview

with

Jones, Denny

(Nickname: Jonesy)

[QUESTION]

JONES: Yes, Carver is my boyfriend.

[QUESTION]

JONES: Well, I woke up that morning after having a really bad dream. I couldn't remember what the dream was, but I remember just feeling awful, you know, just feeling like the world had ended. And then later that day, Carver was off duty and we were hanging out.

[QUESTION]

JONES: We were watching a movie, kind of spooning there, on the couch. And you can see all of downtown from that window, and we were looking at the TV, so we both saw it, just this flash of light, and then this huge ball of smoke rising into the sky. And then I remembered my dream.

[QUESTION]

JONES: My dream was that I was hanging out with Carver and we saw a huge ball of smoke in the sky and then he got an all-call. And then he went off to help and he died. And so I remembered all of this from the dream even before the all-call came in just a second later. So I knew what was going to happen.

[QUESTION]

JONES: Of course. I pleaded with him to ignore the all-call, to stay with me. I knew it was useless but I begged him not to go. I even told him that if he went, our relationship was over, that I wouldn't see him again.

[QUESTION]

JONES: I guess I didn't have time to explain about the dream, although I don't know if it would have helped. Carver doesn't believe in premonitions or superstitions— he's leery of anything that could be just one more illusion, which is one of the many things I love about him. He's just very real. Very direct. But anyway, I only had the amount of time it takes for Carver to put on his suit and he's pretty fast at it, and I guess I panicked. I couldn't think of anything better to do than to beg him to stay. I'm not clever in a crisis. [PAUSE] In retrospect, I realize I could have hidden his boots.

[QUESTION]

JONES: Naturally, he wouldn't listen to me. As soon as the door slammed, I knew. I knew I'd never see him again.

Customer Comment Card

Date: ███████

I was saved by: _Tamara_

I would want to be saved by this Superhero again.
Strongly agree Agree No opinion Disagree Strongly disagree
    O   O   O   ⊘   O

I would recommend this Superhero in the future.
Strongly agree Agree No opinion Disagree Strongly disagree
    O   O   O   O   ⊕

After I was saved, I received counsel about my health and personal safety options.
(Yes)   No

Comments

As an off-duty EMT, I was doing what I could to be useful after several Superheroes had battled some fire ball-throwing Villain. I was administering light burn treatment to Garrote using supplies from his utility belt when I heard Tamara shout something like, "Asana — heat shield," and suddenly my vision clouded for a second. Tamara threw me to the ground and covered me with her body, and then a tremendous blast occurred. I'm assuming that Asana protected us with some sort of heat shield, and Tamara explained to me after I recovered much later that she covered me with her body because her costume was made of a heat-resistant and flame-retardant material. I do not object to having been protected by the heat shield

Over →

or by Tamara's body shield. I do wish to complain about the rude manner in which I was thrown to the ground. Naturally, if any other Superhero were to have saved me then I wouldn't be complaining. On short notice, people must sometimes be thrown to the ground in order to save them (if you are a Superhero). However, isn't Tamara supposed to be able to see the future? Couldn't she have just told me there was going to be a blast far enough ahead of time for me to be able to move to the ground without my cell phone being damaged in the process? Furthermore, when I stated my dislike for the way I was treated, Tamara explained that her powers had been "out of control lately" and that she "just didn't see it coming soon enough." Well, I don't buy that for a second! Let me offer my own assessment: Tamara's laziness got the better of her and she wasn't paying attention to obviously critical future events. I have no doubt that my life was saved by her actions, but I do not believe it was necessary for my cell phone to have been damaged.

Furthermore, if Superheroes who can tell the future are allowed to procrastinate with their critical information, then I'm afraid the bad guys have won. Not to mention, if I threw people to the ground unnecessarily before administering emergency medical care, I would be fired without debate. I hope that Tamara will soon be given the same treatment. Thank you for your time.

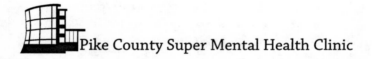 Pike County Super Mental Health Clinic

PATIENT NAME: Tamara
CASE NO.: 5,470,027
BUILDING NO.: 7
DATE OF EVALUATION: 9/14/2010
DATE OF REPORT: 9/16/2010

REASON FOR EVALUATION: The patient is a
35-year-old Superhero with a change in super
powers.

HISTORY OF PRESENT ILLNESS: The patient says
she has been experiencing a shift in the range of
her super powers. In the past, her future-sight
has maintained a range of between 20 minutes
and a few days into the future. Approximately
one year ago, a shift expanded the range to
between 15 minutes and several months into
the future. Gradually, the range increased to
between 5 minutes and 50 years, until yesterday.
Yesterday, just after a confrontation with a villain,
the range suddenly shifted to between just a
few seconds and perhaps hundreds of years into
the future. Because of the wide range of future
history to "sift through," the patient was nearly
unable to detect a future attack from a second
villain in time to defend against it.

MEDICATIONS: None.

ALLERGIES: Morphine and Demerol.

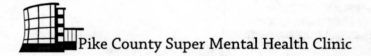Pike County Super Mental Health Clinic

MENTAL STATUS EVALUATION: Despite having recently suffered from a slight concussion and mild burns from a blast, the patient seems alert and focused. The patient makes regular eye contact and speaks coherently. On the scene of the incident yesterday, the patient maintained composure during her power shift while calling for the implementation of a heat shield, shielding a civilian with her body, and dialing an all-call alert to all off-duty Superheroes, all within seconds before the blast hit.

PSYCHIC STATUS EVALUATION: No psychic evaluator was available.

RECOMMENDATIONS: Full evaluation incomplete due to emergency call. Follow-up evaluation recommended, but not yet scheduled.

Poetry from Prison Contest Entry
Title: Unconscious
Author: Mike Barovich
███ █████ ████████ntiary
████ █████████ █████
███████████████,, ████████)

Unconscious

I did it.
I blasted them all.
Tamara and Jerboa are unconscious on the pavement.
Sallah is hanging by his cape from a street light...
        Unconscious.
Asana and Garrote lie at the bottom of a brick wall...
        Unconscious.
Protea's leg and arm dangle from a
fourth story construction platform...
        Unconscious.
It was easy.

I hear a bus engine, several city blocks away.
I see it pass for just a second.
It doesn't stop but it leaves someone behind:

Praxis.

Here's a list of Praxis's recent accomplishments:
- Captured 7 bank robbers singlehandedly.
- Convinced a kidnapper to surrender, kids unharmed.
- Rescued 35 senior citizens from a blazing inferno.
- Defused a bomb attached to a moving roller coaster.
- Taught a kitten how to climb down from a tree by itself.

...And that's just in the last two weeks.

Here's a list of Praxis's known super powers:

?

I think to myself, *this is interesting.*

Praxis walks toward me, slowly. Not like someone with a distinct purpose, but more like someone out for a stroll. Like, Praxis just happened to be there. I feel like saying, "Hey, how's it goin'?"

So I wait. I could blast the Level X Superhero, sure. I could blast the most powerful Superhero in the county. But part of me just wants to see where this is going. Part of me wants to find out how this Level X Superhero without any super powers is going to deal with me.

Praxis gets about 20 feet away and pulls out a rubber band.

I'm about to blast my first Level X Superhero but the rubber band stops me.

Seriously? A rubber band? You're going to fight me with a rubber band? I just blasted your whole team of Superheroes and you're going to defeat me with a rubber band?

And then, Praxis does just that.

And when I regain consciousness, I'm a whole new person.

How a Single Rubber Band Unraveled Mike Barovich's Plan

1.   Praxis removes rubber band from utility belt. Flicks it at Sallah.
2.   Sallah is hanging by his cape on a lamp post. He regains consciousness when the rubber band hits him. Praxis points toward Protea.
3.   Protea is unconscious and situated precariously on a fourth floor construction plank. She falls from the plank, but is caught mid-air by Sallah, who teleports her to safety.

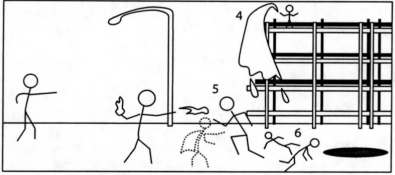

4.   From her new vantage point on the rooftop, Protea is directed by Praxis to spray water at the unconscious Superheroes to wake them up.
5.   Garrote wakes up and charges Mike Barovich. Barovich shoots a fire ball, but Sallah teleports Garrote away before it hits.
6.   Jerboa wakes up.

7. Asana wakes up and charges Barovich. Barovich shoots a fire ball, but Jerboa swoops in, grabs Asana, and flies her away before the fire ball hits.
8. Praxis directs Protea to spray water into the hole where Alabaster Wight is trapped.
9. Alabaster Wight's hole fills with water quickly. He swims to the top and climbs out.

10. Garrote, Asana, Sallah, and Jerboa distract Barovich for a few moments while Alabaster Wight sneaks up behind him.
11. Barovich is knocked unconscious from a light slap by Alabaster Wight.

From Behind Bars

Recaptured and back to bloggin'
9/16/2010 10:58:00 AM

In my last blog, I hinted that I might have something special going on, and as many of you guessed, it was indeed an escape attempt. And as you may have heard, I was captured by a bunch of Superheroes. Best thing that ever happened to me. Seriously! :)

Just a few short days ago, my entire reason for existing was to take revenge on Carver for killing my dad. So, I managed to escape and get a plan together to lure Carver out into the open where I could strike.

However, the plan failed. As a last resort, I popped a lethal dose of pills in my mouth so I could hold off the Superheroes until Carver showed up.

Of course, as you all know 'cause it's all over the internet, Praxis showed up and basically knocked me out with a single rubber band. Somehow, I wound up unconscious in a hospital bed. I've watched all the video footage on the web and I still don't know what happened. :-/

So here's the thing: I didn't expect to be alive this long. Seems one of the Superheroes healed me and reduced the otherwise-lethal effects of the drugs I took. I would have OD'd for sure without her help! :)

And so, as things stand, one Superhero took my dad's life away. And another Superhero gave me a new life. It's strange to say it, but I'm calling us even. It's like an odd sort of cosmic click just happened and everything is back in place. I feel like I can breathe now. :D

All of a sudden, I've taken a good hard look at myself. I can now admit that my dad was whacked out on his experimental drugs, and that toward the end, his <u>beautiful, intelligent mind</u> was shooting off to crazyland. :(

The brain damage prevented him from realizing that what he was doing was wrong. It was Carver's duty to stop him and unfortunately my father was killed in the process. In a way, it makes perfect sense that Carver would have to resort to extremes because my dad was just that tough!

So here I am, back in prison, and, thanks to Asana, probably in better health than when I broke out. It's like I'm a brand new person. I'm back in the poetry workshop class and I'm really churning out some solid stuff! :D

Wish me luck!

Posted in: <u>Drama</u>

Comments:

<u>Standing Tall</u>   9/16/2010 11:14:52 AM
Way to go! Turning your life around is the first step toward taking a new direction!

> <u>Admin</u>   9/16/2010 11:15:28 AM
> Thanks, Standing Tall. I appreciate the positive comment.

<u>here4ever</u>   9/16/2010 11:17:49 AM
If it were me, I'd still be after Carver. Maybe that's why I haven't made parole yet LOL!

> <u>Admin</u>   9/16/2010 11:21:44 AM
> It's never too late to change, here4. Carver and I did have one quick conversation. We told each other we were sorry about the way things were, and I'm not afraid to admit it felt good to acknowledge what's between us. That said, it's not like I'll be inviting him to any barbeques.

The Civilized Foundation

Onward, to True Civilization™!

A joint venture
by Jake Bonson and Lage

"A perfect system never counts
on its own perfection."

Mission Statement
The Civilized Foundation's mission is to develop artificial models that simulate theoretical conditions for a truly civilized way of life in an effort to find a working alternative to current systems of government.

The Civilized Foundation is Pro-Civilization!

Our theoretical models show that no matter how you try to eliminate organized civilizational structures, there will always be someone willing and capable of exploiting the resulting conditions through the creation of negatively-impacting social structure. The Civilized Foundation creates and manipulates variables in models in an effort to discover the magical formula for True Civilization.

What is True Civilization?

It's a world in which you are the master of your world, and every other person is the master of theirs. Can it happen? Our theoretical models say there is a 28.57% chance and climbing!

Progress Report

When the Civilized Foundation first got started, our theoretical models could only predict a 7.49% chance of True Civilization. Now, our theoretical models have increased that probability to 28.57% and we continue to make progress toward our goal of 40% by the end of 2012!

Message from the Civilized Foundation's founder, Lage:

"Hi. I used to want to destroy civilization. My systematic analysis of all current systems of government had revealed to me that they were fundamentally flawed because of built-in tendencies to allow negatively-impacting exploitation to occur. Thus, I felt the only responsible thing to do was turn into a criminal bent on destroying civilization. But then I ran into some Superheroes that cared. Level X Superhero Praxis took the time to connect me with Jake Bonson, who was able to demonstrate using convincing data and simulation programming that a drastic policy change in civilizational structure will result in a further degradation of the ideals of my cause (True Civilization). Bonson's data showed that without a civilizational structure in place, someone will inevitably create a negatively-impacting exploitive one. I started the Civilized Foundation to answer the call of True Civilization: to design a theoretical civilizational structure that can guard against negatively-impacting exploitation. Now I'm working toward that goal by helping to create a better theoretical future using models that express the probability of True Civilization occurring within certain given parameters! I also took anger management classes."

Contact the Civilized Foundation* to make a donation or find out how else you can help:

true.civilization@gmail.com

*The majority of the staff of the Civilized Foundation are allowed to check e-mail on Mondays and Thursdays if they have maintained Good Behavior status.

Disclaimer: The Civilized Foundation does not advocate anarchy or any other currently known system or non-system for organized or disorganized government.

[QUESTION]

JONES: Carver knocked on my door about three minutes later, three minutes after he left to respond to the all-call.

[QUESTION]

JONES: Well, at first I thought it was someone about to tell me that Carver was dead but then I was like, 'That's way too soon.' And then I thought it was the guy across the hall who always has to borrow flour or soy sauce or something and he always has to borrow it when he knows Carver isn't around. So I ignored the door until the third knock.

[QUESTION]

JONES: Well, yes, Carver had a key. He just wanted to be dramatic. [LAUGHS] It's hard loving a Superhero. You have to be strong in ways that you don't even think are possible at first. But eventually you get used to it. And you get stronger. And it grows on you. And you start to wonder how you ever lived without it.

[QUESTION]

JONES: The challenge, I guess. At some point, you have to accept that you're not cut out for it but that you're going to do it anyway. I guess it's kind of like being a Superhero.

Level X

Name:	ID:
County: **Pike County**	Date:

How to fill out this form:
- For multiple choice questions, completely fill the box to the left of your choice.
- For write-in answers, please print legibly in the space provided.

In Document K, were Asana and Auslander disobeying River Waters Mandate Statute 125.0108?

- ☐ I do not have authorization to view the River Waters Mandate Statutes.
- ☐ I cannot answer this question without violating River Waters Mandate Statute 24.118.
- ☐ The River Waters Mandate doesn't have statutes.
- ☐ The River Waters Mandate was never approved.
- ☐ The River Waters Mandate isn't real.

If Superheroes were allowed to become free agents within the Superhero industry, which of the following Superheroes would licensed Superhero agent Reuben most want to represent?

- ☐ Alabaster Wight
- ☐ Asana
- ☐ Carver
- ☐ Garrote
- ☐ Jerboa
- ☐ Praxis
- ☐ Protea
- ☐ Pulmo
- ☐ Sallah
- ☐ Tamara

Which of the following characters from Document X is most likely to commit a crime in the future?

- ☐ Lage
- ☐ Mike Barovich
- ☐ The EMT

In Document X, why did Praxis orchestrate the victory through the other Superheroes, instead of resolving the situation alone?

- ☐ Praxis has no super powers and is therefore helpless without the team.
- ☐ Praxis wants to encourage teamwork.
- ☐ Praxis doesn't like showing off.
- ☐ That was the only way Praxis could have resolved the situation.
- ☐ Praxis made use of the simplest solution to the problem.
- ☐ There was never any situation to resolve.
- ☐ Other:

_____

_____

_____

_____

Continued on other side

Which of the following best describes your understanding of
the Superheroes depicted within the files used for Psychological
Assessments I through X?
- ☐ They are real Superheroes and no names have been changed.
- ☐ They are real Superheroes but their names have been
  changed.
- ☐ They are subjective representations of real Superheroes.
- ☐ They are fictions created to aid in the psychological
  assessment of Superheroes.
- ☐ There is no psychological assessment.

Of the characters from Documents W and X, which of them is the
most invulnerable?
- ☐ Alabaster Wight
- ☐ Asana
- ☐ Carver
- ☐ Edward
- ☐ Garrote
- ☐ Jake Bonson
- ☐ Jerboa
- ☐ Jonesy
- ☐ Lage
- ☐ Maya
- ☐ Mike Barovich
- ☐ Nelson
- ☐ Pierre Gourmont
- ☐ Praxis
- ☐ Protea
- ☐ Pulmo
- ☐ Sallah
- ☐ Tamara
- ☐ The EMT
- ☐ All of the above are equally invulnerable.

Explain your answer to the previous question.

_____

_____

_____

_____

_____

Acknowledgements

My family, Caroline Albert, Lavell Allen, Lars Bakken,
Tara Bannon Williamson, Elizabeth Beeson,
Matthew Brandon, Jessica Brown, Lorrie Ann Butler,
Jeremy Chapman, Shaina Cohen, Kristofer Collins,
Adam Cousins, Corrine Davis, Ri del Rio,
the Denver Public Library, Desi, Megan Ellis,
Olivia Emery, Jonathan Evison, Arianne Garden Vazquez,
Frank Greer, Chris Hammersley, Sean Hansz, Pat Hodapp,
Lauren Hoffman, Brian Howard, Jill Hutchinson,
Michelle Jeffrey Delk, Michelle Jeske, Shawn Kilburn,
the King County Library System, Josh Knisely, *KNOCK*,
Joaquin Liebert, Pei-Yu Lin, Brad Listi,
Robyn McGimsey, Scotty McMullan, Collin Moon,
Kristen Mullin Bakken, Aimee and Joey Nelson,
everyone at TheNervousBreakdown.com,
Shoun Otis and *Needles for Teeth*, Heather Pengilly-Dorn,
James Peters, Martin Piccoli, Charlie Potter, Dave Prosper,
Rachel, Alex Reed, Anneliese Rix, Rebecca Ross,
the Seattle Public Library, Angela Sigg, Elizabeth Smith,
Bryan Tomasovich, Erik Tosten, David Trabosh,
the Winchester people, Marc Wiseman,
and everyone in the writer's groups.

"Support" first appeared in *KNOCK* #10.

Printed in the U.S.A. by Lightning Source on acid-free, 30%
post-consumer content recycled paper.

Emergency Press participates in the Green Press Initiative.
The mission of the Green Press Initiative is to work with
book and newspaper industry stakeholders to conserve
natural resources, preserve endangered forests, reduce
greenhouse gas emissions, and minimize impacts on
indigenous communities.

Books from Emergency Press

Slut Lullabies, by Gina Frangello
ISBN 978-0-9753623-7-2, Paperback, $15.00

American Junkie, by Tom Hansen
ISBN 978-0-9753623-6-5, Paperback, $15.00

IMPATIENCE, a Poem in 52 Pieces by Scott Zieher
ISBN 978-0-9753623-5-8, Paperback, $15.00

Touched by Lightning, by Ernest Loesser
ISBN 978-0-9753623-4-1, Paperback, $15.00

The Border Will Be Soon: Meditations on the Other Side,
   by Chad Faries
ISBN 0-9753623-3-X, Paperback, $15.00

Six Trips in Two Directions, by Jayson Iwen
ISBN 0-9753623-2-1, Paperback, $15.00

VIRGA, a Poem by Scott Zieher
ISBN 0-9753623-1-3, Paperback, $15.00

Emergency Press
emergencypress.org
press@emergencypress.org

Aaron Dietz is an instructional designer for online high schools and has written courses in game modding, computer programming, green design, and 3-D video games. It's natural for him to write quizzes. He's worked a decade in libraries. He's also been paid to count traffic.

aarondietz.us